HAWK AMONG THE SPARROWS

HAWK AMONG THE SPARROWS

three science fiction novellas

Dean McLaughlin

Charles Scribner's Sons · New York

The stories in this book were first
published in *Astounding Science Fiction*
and/or its successor, *Analog Science Fiction—Science Fact.*

Copyright © 1976, 1968, 1964, 1960 Dean McLaughlin

Library of Congress Cataloging in Publication Data

McLaughlin, Dean.   Hawk among the sparrows.
  1. Science fiction, American.   I. Title.
PZ4.M16155Haw [PS3563.A31794] 813'.0876 76–38
ISBN 0–684–14577–4

1 3 5 7 9 11 13 15 17 19 c/c 20 18 16 14 12 10 8 6 4 2

Printed in the United States of America

Contents

Introduction
TOURING THE WORKSHOP

One of the most commonplace "explanations" of science fiction is to say that the writer begins with the question "What if . . . ?" (What if a man could travel in time, from one age to another? What if critters from Mars—or someplace Out There—invaded this earth of ours? A nod to the ghost of H.G. Wells.)

It sounds reasonable, but I am inclined to quibble. What sounds "reasonable" is not automatically correct, and, besides, I haven't made a story that way in twenty-five years at the trade.

It is possible that some of my colleagues have used this approach. I have not asked. But for me, a story has usually started at a slightly later point in the chain of thought, with the observation that, given the "what if" situation, certain consequences would follow.

A distinction without a difference? Perhaps. Which is why I call it a quibble instead of a disagreement. But it is out of just such careful distinctions that a science fiction story can be made.

And a good science fiction story is, indeed, made, not born. A question frequently asked is, "Where do you get your ideas?"—as if there were some secret storehouse where they are found. The prosaic truth, though, is that ideas come from almost anywhere, and, in my experience,

3

rarely the same source twice. Once it was an item in the letter column of *Time* magazine. Once it was a paragraph in a book on recent discoveries in geology. Perhaps the idea I feel most smug about came from a note in *SFWA Forum*, a casual publication circulated among members of Science Fiction Writers of America—an item which reported a singularly intriguing clause in a certain publisher's standard contract. None of my fellows, I suspect, gave it a second thought; I saw a story in it.

Ideas are plentiful. The universe is full of them. And the science fiction writer has an infinity of possible universes to invent, exploit, and explore. The real problem is to know a good idea when it plugs itself into the mind. And then the hard part comes, the paper work; taking the raw material and developing it into a presentable story. Hopefully, a great one.

Another popular misconception, though not one held by those truly familiar with science fiction, is that the writer must have a deep and extensive knowledge of science. This does help, sometimes. For the subcategory "hard" science fiction, best exemplified by Hal Clement's *Mission of Gravity*, it is virtually indispensable. But it can also be a serious handicap. Ray Bradbury's Mars, as presented in *The Martian Chronicles*, was preposterous even in the late 1940s when the stories were written, and the visions of the Mariner probes have helped not at all. The stories remain fine stories, but they must be read with the understanding that where Bradbury wrote "Mars," the reader must substitute "Neverland." A symbolic Mars, a counter-Earth, a foil for the follies of mankind.

Much science fiction, in fact, makes use of fairly standard, off-the-shelf ingredients. Spaceships, matter transmitters, communication devices, time transporters, and antigravity machines—to name only a few—are all familiar to the science fiction reader and need not be anatomized unless, for reasons of his own, the author wants to call attention to some special point of interest. And more than one item of hardware—or software, for that matter—is described more in terms of what it can do than of how it does the job.

And while a number of science fiction writers are of considerable scientific achievement and even eminence— the English astrophysicist Sir Fred Hoyle immediately comes to mind—there remain many others of more humble education. Among those known to me, several very well known science fiction authors never went beyond high school. Others are, at least by training, lawyers, public relations counselors, journalists, architects, and retired naval officers. More than a few took their university degrees in literature; I did so myself. One—a particularly good friend—holds a doctorate in musicology.

This is not to imply that science fiction writers as a class are ignorant of science. Quite apart from their formal education, some are and some are not. My point is that accurate, detailed scientific knowledge is not an essential ingredient.

I have meant the foregoing to illuminate both the strengths and some of the failings of the stories in this volume. I would prefer that the stories be read first, before the commentary that follows. The stories were written to stand by themselves, without explanation or justification except such as is within them. What follows would probably make more sense if the stories were already known, just as a tour of the workshop is more understandable if one knows what came out of it.

"Hawk Among the Sparrows" is the most recently written and, ironically, the one most out-of-date in some of its details. France has long since moved her nuclear test grounds to the South Pacific. General De Gaulle is no longer on the scene. Such discrepancies could be patched; the Egyptians might be testing *their* bombs. Another French president as prickly as the old general could be introduced (though he would need a bit of explanation). Five years hence I would have to do the job again. One of the special hazards of the science fiction business.

"Hawk" is also the story which took longest to grow. One of its roots goes back to an editorial John Campbell wrote for *Astounding Science Fiction* in 1948, in which he speculated about what French aeronautical experts circa the first World War would have made of a ramjet-powered aircraft, had one fallen into their hands. The engine would be essentially an open-ended tube with fuel injectors and an ignition device. It would be far beyond the state of their art. They would have been fuddled.

Another suggestion came to me when I read that, for the Hiroshima bombing, the superfortress *Enola Gay* was stripped of all armament except her tail guns. The gain in airspeed by thus lightening and streamlining the bomber was deemed more important than defense against Japanese interceptors; part of the argument being that, if the bomber were attacked from any direction but the rear, the opposed velocities of bomber and fighter would permit no more than three bullets to hit the plane, an acceptable risk.

Years later, I was reminded of this while reading about midair collisions. One factor contributing to the frequency thereof (all that sky, how come they're always running into each other?) was, I was informed, that a pilot's visual acuity was thus-and-such, and his reaction time was x fractions of a second, during which a Mach 1 aircraft will have flown xyz miles. By the time the pilots of two such aircraft flying head-on toward each other could recognize their danger and act on it, it would be too late. Obviously, it seemed to me, a Mach 2 jet and, say, a World War I biplane would hardly have time for so much as a nodding acquaintance.

These bits of curiosa stayed in my head for years, interesting but useless, until a copy of Quentin Reynolds's *They Fought for the Sky* came into my hands. It could as well have been any of a dozen other books about the aerial-combat phase of World War I. It seemed obvious, as I read, that the history of that time had been at the root of much 1930s-style science fiction, especially the sub-genre known as space opera.

Things began to come together. At some point the notion became more than casual, back-of-the-brain thinking. I began putting a story together.

Here I should mention two "sources" which, though they might seem obvious, could not have affected my thinking. Long after "Hawk" was published, my attention was called to a piece by Art Buchwald. In it, the humorist/satirist proposed—tongue firmly cheeked, as usual—the World War I vintage SPAD as the perfect aircraft for use in Vietnam. The piece was originally published some years before "Hawk" was written, but I had not seen it or known of it. Which is just as well: Buchwald anticipated me on any number of details.

The other non-source was the "Peanuts" comic strip, in which, at the same time I was writing, a very Walter Mittyish beagle named Snoopy flew numerous missions (usually atop his doghouse) against the oft-cursed Red Baron. I did not see the strips until later, when they appeared in book form. I enjoyed them greatly.

Sources that may have had an effect would have to include Mark Twain's *A Connecticut Yankee in King Arthur's Court*, and L. Sprague de Camp's *Lest Darkness Fall*, both of which I had read years before and much

admired. Interestingly (and perhaps not entirely coinci-
dentally) neither of these authors wasted any great effort
(as Wells did) in explaining how their heroes arrived at
the time and place they found themselves. Neither did I.

In my own case, it was simply a feeling that the fact of
a transposition in time would be sufficient, without
trundling out elaborate (and largely specious) explanations of how the job was done. Among other considera-
tions, I could point to a long line of literary precedent
(including the aforementioned, which is more than they
could do) amounting almost to a tradition. In each case,
the transposition is accomplished with what amounts to a
wave of the magic wand, after which the hero is where
the author wants him and the story is under way.
(Happening later in the story, it would seem more gratui-
tous and would require far more elaborate justification.)

So I had an idea for a story. But even then I felt no
haste to begin the paper work. Other projects had my
attention. Then, early in 1967 (for reasons complex,
trivial, and unrelated) I felt persuaded to take a short
break from the novel then in progress (which now still
waits, up there on the shelf) to write a "quick short
story."

It took eleven months, and the story was anything but
short when I finished. I got interested. Like a kid with an
old clock.

It was not all easy going, though. There were several
false starts while I groped for the right place and the right
way to begin. Beginnings are hard. And there were
hangups later on, such as the point where I searched all
the sources at hand for the instruments to be found in a
Nieuport's cockpit. And I still have only hints and
hunches as to when and where the Molotov cocktail was
invented. (Finland? Spain?)

Early on, I discovered that I had an idea and a situation

that were fundamentally comic. Anachronisms could hardly be avoided. And some aspects of early aviation are, from our superior point of view, hopelessly ludicrous. The rotary engine, standard at the time, seems now a preposterous way to fly an "aeroplane"; yet for its time it was a reasonable, logical, and efficient solution to the problem of building a lightweight motor powerful enough to get an aircraft off the ground. Turn-and-bank indicators consisted of just such crude improvisations as I describe; I also understand that they did not work very well.

Other aspects of the story were not humorous at all. It was a time when men were killed, often very unpleasantly. Many accounts of that time speak of men who jumped from burning planes. They did not have parachutes. I can imagine few acts more desperate—more desolate of hope. And the belief held by so many that they fought a war to end wars for all time has become, now, merely pathetic.

In writing "Hawk," I did not feel I could avoid either the comedy or the tragedy inherent in the material. I did not try.

Pika-Don's flight capabilities were adopted, for the most part, from the real-world capabilities of the Lockheed SR-71 "Blackbird," with one significant addition. The SR-71 is a truly jaw-dropping piece of hardware, and I did not need to exaggerate on most details, though I suspect its turning radius is far larger than *Pika-Don*'s. But, like most high-powered jet aircraft, the SR-71 requires a conventional runway—good hard pavement, and lots of it. Such a requirement could not be met by any airfield circa 1918. I therefore bestowed on my fictional superplane a vertical takeoff and landing capability, such as is enjoyed by the British Harrier interceptor which was unveiled within a year of the time "Hawk" was written. (I had read of such developments in the works, so I was not surprised; neither can I make any claims of prediction. So much for the technical ingenuity of at least one science fiction writer.)

The title? Originally, it was a metaphor somewhere in the story's interior. I chopped it out and moved it up front when I saw how apt it was, how well it fitted. (Giving credit where due, though, I was aware of Agatha Christie's mystery *Cat Among the Pigeons*, though I have never read it, and used a similarly structured phrase.)

The version appearing here is substantially the same as that originally published. I have corrected a few small factual errors, added a detail or two, and sharpened a few points. Otherwise, in spite of some temptation to "improve," I have left it as it was.

"The Permanent Implosion" was more quickly schemed and promptly written. It was plotted almost completely while I was driving home from a party in Evanston. Riding with me was Howard DeVore, well-known science fiction fan, collector, and dealer in old-and-rare and/or old-and-grubby; sometimes known to initiates as Big Hearted Howard.

The party had abounded with science fiction people, was hosted, in fact, by a staffer of a recently formed publishing house whose line included more than a little of the genre. In the course of the festivities, Howard had learned of a plan by the publisher for a series of anthologies of previously unpublished stories—essentially a magazine in paperback form.

A writer is always interested in new markets. This one sounded good. At the time, it was an almost-new idea. (As it happened, though, the project was stillborn.) The thought of doing a story for this new book/magazine came to me almost by reflex. I began bouncing thoughts off Howard's ears.

One device for creating a story out of virtually nothing —one I had found fruitful in the past—is to pick out a "standard" science fiction situation which has not been used for some time. I reached into the catalog and pulled one out: matter transmission.

Some ten-odd years before, Lester del Rey had published a novelette, "The Wind Between the Worlds." An accident with an interstellar matter transmitter created the wind referred to in the title. So far as I knew, nothing similar to that idea had been used before or since. I felt there was a lot of mileage left in it.

Even as I took hold of it, the concept began to change shape. All of del Rey's story fell away—I didn't recall the plot very well. Even the matter-transmitter aspect vanished. My own story began to grow from the lopped-off root. What sort of man might be called on to deal with such a problem? What would motivate him to accept the task? How could the problem be solved?

By the time I got home, I was ready to start work.

Here again, I found myself working with a basically comic idea. But while "Hawk" was a comedy of logical consequences, "Implosion" was a comedy of absurd premise.

In the mid-1940s *Astounding Science Fiction* had included a feature called "Probability Zero." This consisted of very short stories whose outstanding quality was logical outrageousness—the sort of thing that might come from a collaboration between Baron Munchausen and Lewis Carroll. Preposterous premises and facetious conclusions were welcome there, and great fun was had by all.

The basic idea of "Implosion" was just such a premise.

While the dramatic situation required that it be played fairly straight, I couldn't be entirely serious about it. Several comic opportunities presented themselves; I couldn't resist. And I found myself indulging in one outrageous metaphor after another, each trying to top the one preceding it.

Another stylistic impulse I found myself yielding to was a constant—sometimes almost sentence by sentence—shift in focus of attention. I convinced myself, once I noticed what I was doing, that it would give the story a sense of movement. True or not, I am in no position to judge; it was what I thought at the time, and how it looked from inside.

Oddly enough, the final permutation of the idea was one of the few points I did not think of during my drive home from Evanston. I think it derived from a letter in a 1945 *Astounding Science Fiction*—I suspect a "Probability Zero" offering left over after the feature was discontinued. In it, George O. Smith reported on an industrial accident in which a vacuum tank exploded, after which residents nearby had vacuum instead of water coming out of their faucets. This was, I felt, just the right twist with which to wind up such a reasonable—given the premise—preposterous tale.

When *Analog* published the story, several readers wrote in. Working from the normal air pressure in the Denver region and the dimensions of the story's insatiable vacuum (as near as they could guess/estimate), they calculated that the wind of infalling air would be no more than a breeze, hardly able to raise a bit of dust at the end of a dry summer, and it would be several million years before we need worry about running out of air. Within the limits of their analysis, they were probably right. But what I had in mind was the effect such a vacuum would have on meteorological conditions; what sort of weather patterns would develop around such a persistent, immobile low-pressure zone. My assumption on this point may have been incorrect—it was an assumption, not a carefully reasoned conclusion, but I wouldn't have had a story without it—and perhaps I had not made my thought sufficiently clear. In their analysis, my critics did not consider meteorological effects.

At least there were no complaints about it as a story. It was great fun in the writing, and of my stories—as seen from inside, which can be a very different point of view—it remains the one I am most satisfied with. Not that I think it to be my best; I know it is not. But it is the one which I believe I came closest to doing everything I set out to do. Other (and, I know, better) stories have aimed higher and, inevitably, have fallen short by a larger measure.

"The Brotherhood of Keepers" is such a piece—one of my most ambitious. And to this day I remain dissatisfied with it. I have been told that it is good—possibly my best ever; certainly it was my best as of the time it first appeared.

And while "Hawk" and "Implosion" grew out of comic ideas and were done with more than a little humor (and perhaps a bit of playfulness), "Brotherhood" was done with high seriousness; what humor can be found in it was mostly inserted after the first draft was done.

"Brotherhood" had two separate origins, and it was only when the parts came together in my mind that I had a story.

I had the setting first. In the late 1940s, Fredric Brown wrote a zany story titled "Placet Is a Crazy Place." Indeed it was. Placet was a planet of a binary star—that is, two stars orbiting around each other. Placet itself orbited around *both* stars—first one, then the other, describing a figure-eight orbit. Years later, recalling the story, I mentioned this rather imaginative detail to my astronomer father. He was not impressed. Such a system, he told me, would not be stable. It could not survive more than a single passage, if that.

But then he added, it *would* be possible for the planet of one star in a binary pair to be captured by the other, provided certain conditions were met. At once I was interested. Would it be possible for such a world to be captured back and forth, first by one, then the other? The answer was a qualified yes. Most likely the event would happen irregularly—the specifics would depend on the orbital elements of all the bodies involved. There would also be a strong possibility of the planet's being thrown into an orbit circling the binary pair's center of gravity, too far from either for life to survive.

A concept such as this is the sort of thing a science fiction writer waits for, hopes for, and goes out looking for. When he finds one, he holds it close to his vest, not even hinting to his colleagues. Lovely stuff. Red meat for the imagination.

But I hadn't the foggiest notion what to do with it. I have always been annoyed by science fiction stories in which a truly unusual setting is used, yet the scenery remains mere scenery and bears no relation to the story. I prefer to have a story grow out of the environment in which it happens, rather than being arbitrarily imposed upon it. So the idea went into my mental file, into the folder tabbed "Hold until it fits something."

As it happened, the wait was not a very long one. Loren Eiseley's speculative, meditative essay "The Fire Apes" came to my hands. I am no longer sure which I discovered first, that essay or his book *The Immense Journey*; I encountered both at about the same time, and I was greatly impressed and stimulated by both. Ever since, I have eagerly reached for any and all of the man's writings that have come my way.

But it was in "The Fire Apes" that I found an idea with which I could not entirely agree. I've learned since that it was, and is, a generally accepted corollary to evolution theory; in his essay Eiseley was merely repeating it. But I had not encountered it before.

Briefly, the idea is this: if, in a given environment, an ecological "niche" is fully occupied and/or exploited by an organism, no other organism can successfully evolve to occupy/exploit that niche. A bit of thought and understanding confirms the general reasonableness of this idea.

But, I thought, the operation of this principle depends on the blind, essentially purposeless forces of the natural world; it would not automatically apply to intelligence, because intelligence permits the exercise of rational choice. Being intelligent, being able to choose, men might perceive another "people" evolving and might choose to permit the process to go on. In that act of choice, I saw the foundations of a story.

And my father's captured and recaptured planet was exactly the sort of place where the story could happen. For on such a planet the pressures of natural selection would be at their most harsh and evolution therefore far more rapid than here on our own relatively placid world. (It was during the ice ages—a terrible time in which to live, and in which many failed to survive—that modern man evolved; many other large mammals died out—quite possibly because man *did* evolve, and then hunted them to extinction.)

Putting the two ingredients together, I had an unusual, interesting setting, and I had a story to tell.

It was a stubborn, refractory story. I wrote an opening scene, then discovered that the only way to give the reader necessary information was to place another scene ahead of it. Later, because I felt the story would be incomplete without them, I was compelled to add the interludes and the epilogue, which for symmetry's sake required also the writing of a prologue. While prologues and epilogues are fairly common, I had seen interludes used only once, in the next-to-last story of Isaac Asimov's Foundation Series. The device served Asimov well. I think it did the same for me.

After the first draft was done, I discovered that I had a scene which was, inadvertently and quite apart from my purpose in writing it, pure slapstick comedy. Since I could not remove the comedy without doing damage, I did the only other thing possible—I added a few more comic moments so the one would not seem out of place. Nor was I satisfied with the ending as it stood, very lamely, in the first draft. I had to devise a new one, one not inconsistent with what went before, unless I wanted to tear down most of what I had done, down to the bare bedplate, and start over. I mulled, gnawed, and fretted, and then found that the thread of comedy I had added late in the game offered also a solution to *that* problem.

Still I was dissatisfied. I always will be dissatisfied. I will admit to this day it was a story I did not finish so much as give up on, unable to do more.

My soon-to-become-intelligent creatures, the floppers, were designed to meet the story's requirements: protean bodies, not so much capable of doing certain things well as they were capable of changing to meet the demands of a radically changing environment. I also wanted to suggest a number of such transitions in their evolutionary past. For if one thing was sure, it was that their world had given their ancestors some terribly cruel challenges.

In the version originally submitted to *Astounding Science Fiction*, the floppers were equipped with only one large eye. Editor John Campbell requested I give them two, arguing that binocular vision was necessary for the development of depth perception (essentially true) and that this, in turn, would be necessary for the evolution of intelligence (a considerably more questionable thesis). I felt that two eyes were uncomfortably anthropomorphic, but I was in a poor position to argue the point; among other things, I had wanted my floppers to possess depth perception with their single eye. I thought that, by one improvisation or another (and evolution is a long sequence of improvisations), it should be possible, although I had not been able to contrive such a mechanism or even to squeeze the idea into the story as a bald assertion. It would have been too obviously "author shows the reader how ingenious he is"—something I prefer not to be consciously guilty of. I made the requested changes.

This stands as still another cause for my lingering dissatisfaction, but either way the result would not have been what I really wanted. What I wanted was beyond my reach. (If I could devise a way to permit monocular depth perception *and* a way to introduce it naturally, without fanfare, into the story, I think I would change it back. But I still don't think I can do it.)

In the end, though, in spite of dissatisfactions, there was still a feeling of considerable accomplishment. In the course of writing, I had found myself closely examining some of the implications of evolution theory. I found myself facing conclusions which made me distinctly uncomfortable, yet which I couldn't evade. On only two other occasions have I found myself wrestling with as strong a theme. One of those times, I had a much clearer view of what I believed; the other time I was not aware when I began what sort of beast I had by the horns and did not discover it until late in the game. In "Brotherhood," I began with at least some inkling of the contest I was taking up. I remain unsure whether I won or met defeat, or even if such terms apply. Whatever, it was an adventure through uncharted territory. And it has been my experience that what comes easy is not valued; what comes hard, even if, in the end, a feeling of imperfectness persists, is to be treasured. "Brotherhood" did not come easy, but it came. In spite of doubts and reservations, I have about it a sense of having done a thing worth doing.

An introduction such as this would stand incomplete without acknowledgment to the many people who have brought me to this place and time. I cannot list them all, let alone identify exactly what part each has added to the pattern. But in addition to the ones already mentioned, a few more should at least be named. In no particular order, they are David and Jane Manwaring; Bruce Wilson; Allan Seager; Pauline Zollar; Frank Reed; Alan Nourse; Harry Altshuler; Dr. S. L. Kellermann; Judith Merril; Damon Knight; Hal Weidner; Lloyd Biggle, Jr.; Frederik Pohl; Patricia Rinaldi; Poul Anderson; James Blish; Gordon Dickson; Larry and Noreen Shaw; Algis Budrys; Karol, Suzi, and Sybil DeVore; Hans Stefan Santesson; Nancy Boersma; Kelly Freas; Robert Heinlein; Harlan Ellison; and, not least, Tim Pike, who said exactly the right thing at the right time. A tip of the hat, a word of gratitude, to all of these and to those others who, by failing memory, have suffered my neglect. Like all men, I am part of all that I have met. My thanks to all of you.

HAWK AMONG THE SPARROWS

The map-position scope on the left side of *Pika-Don*'s instrument panel showed where he was, but it didn't show airfields. Right now, Howard Farman needed an airfield. He glanced again at the fuel gauge. Not a chance of making it to Frankfurt, or even into West Germany. Far below, white clouds like a featureless ocean sprawled all the way to the horizon.

Those clouds shouldn't have been there. Less than four hours ago, before he lifted off the *Eagle*, he'd studied a set of weather satellite photos freshly televised down from orbit. Southern France had been almost clear—only a dotting of cottonboll tufts. It should not have been possible for solid overcast to build up so fast. For the dozenth time, he flipped through the meteorological data on his clipboard. No, nothing that could have created such a change.

That made two things he hadn't been able to figure out. The second was even stranger. He'd lifted from the *Eagle*'s deck at midmorning. The French bomb test he'd been snooping had blinded him for a while—how long he didn't know—and *Pika-Don* was thrown out of control. The deadman circuit had cut in; control was re-established. When his sight came back—and it couldn't have

21

been terribly long—the sun had been halfway down in the west.

It wasn't possible. *Pika-Don* didn't carry enough fuel to stay up that long.

Just the same, she had stayed up, and she still had almost half her load. When he couldn't find the *Eagle* near Gibraltar, he'd thought there was enough to take him to the American airbase at Frankfurt. (And where could the *Eagle* have gone? What could have happened to her radar beacon? Could the French blast have smashed *Pika-Don*'s reception equipment? Everything else seemed to work all right. But he'd made an eyeball search, too. Aircraft tenders didn't just vanish.)

On the map scope, the Rhone valley crawled slowly southward under the north-moving central piplight that marked *Pika-Don*'s inertially computed position. It matched perfectly the radar-scanned terrain displayed on the airspace viewscope on the right-hand side of the instrument panel. Frankfurt was still beyond the horizon, more than four hundred miles off. *Pika-Don* didn't have fuel to cover half that distance.

Well, he wouldn't find an airfield by staying up here, above that carpet of cloud. He eased the throttles back and put *Pika-Don*'s nose down. She'd burn fuel a lot faster down close to the deck, but at Mach 1.5 he could search a lot of ground before the tanks went dry.

Not that he absolutely had to find an airfield. *Pika-Don* could put down almost anywhere if she had to. But an airfield would make it a lot simpler to get a new load of fuel, and it would make less complicated the problems that would come from putting down in a technically still friendly nation.

It was a long way down. He watched the radar-echo altimeter reel downward like a clock thrown into panicked reverse; watched the skin temperature gauge edge up, level out, edge up again as *Pika-Don* descended into thicker air. For the first eighty thousand feet, visibility was perfect, but at twelve thousand feet *Pika-Don* went into the clouds; it was like being swallowed by gray night. Uneasily, Farman watched the radar horizon; these clouds might go down all the way to the ground, and at Mach 1.5 there wouldn't be anything left but a smear if *Pika-Don* hit. She was too sweet an airplane for that. Besides, he was inside.

He broke out into clear air a little under four thousand feet. A small city lay off to his right. He turned toward it. Beaufort, the map scope said. There ought to be some sort of airfield near it. He pulled the throttles back as far as he dared—just enough to maintain airspeed. The Machmeter slipped back to 1.25.

He passed north of the town, scanning the land. No sign of a field. He circled southward, careful to keep his bearing away from the town's center. There'd be trouble enough about his coming down in France—aerial trespass by a nuclear-armed warplane, to start with—without half the townspeople screaming about smashed windows, cracked plaster, and roosters so frightened they stopped laying eggs. The ambassador in Paris was going to earn his paycheck this week.

Still no airfield. He went around again, farther out. Dozens of villages flashed past below. He tore his flight plan, orders, and weather data off their clipboard—crammed the papers into the disposal funnel; wouldn't do to have nosy Frenchmen pawing that stuff, not at all. He substituted the other flight plan—the one they'd given him just in case he had to put down in French or French-friendly territory.

He was starting his third circuit and the fuel gauge was leaning against the red mark when he saw the field. It wasn't much of a place—just a grassy postage stamp with a few old planes in front of three ramshackle sheds and a windsock flopping clumsily over the middle one. He put around, aimed for it, and converted to vertical thrust. Airspeed dropped quickly—there was a momentary surge of wing-surface heating—and then he was hovering only a few miles from the field. He used the deflectors to cover the distance, losing altitude as he went. He jockeyed to a position near the hangars, faced *Pika-Don* into the wind, and let her down.

The engines died—starved of fuel—before he could cut them off.

It took a while to disconnect all the umbilici that linked him into *Pika-Don*'s control and environment systems. Some of the connections were hard to reach. It took a while longer to raise the canopy, climb over the side, and drop to the ground. Two soldiers were waiting for him. They had rifles.

The bigger one—the one with the bushy mustache—spoke dangerously. Farman didn't know French, but their gestures with rifle muzzles were a universal language. He raised his hands. "I'm an American," he said. "I ran out of fuel." He hoped they weren't disciples of the late *grand Charles*. They looked nasty enough.

The two exchanged glances. *"Américain?"* the smaller one asked. He was clean-shaved. His eyes had a deep, hollow look. He didn't sound at all displeased.

Farman nodded vigorously. "Yes. American." He pointed to the fifty-one-star flag on his coverall sleeve. Their faces broke into delighted smiles and they turned their gun muzzles groundward. The small one—he made Farman think of a terrier, and his rifle was absurdly big for him—pointed to a shack beyond the hangars.

At least the natives seemed friendly. Farman went. The area in front of the hangars had been paved—an uneven spread of asphalt. Half a dozen rattletrap airplanes stood in a line, facing out toward the field. Where the pavement met unpaved ground, it was one mud puddle after another. Farman had to be careful where he put his feet; his flight boots had been clean when he took off this morning. The soldiers didn't seem to mind. They splashed cheerfully through the wet and scuffed their heels on the tufts of grass.

The planes were all the same type—biplanes with open cockpits and two-bladed wooden propellers and radial-type piston engines. The kind of planes, Farman thought, that shouldn't even be flying any more. Nevertheless, they were obviously working airplanes, with oil stains on their cowls and the smell of gasoline and patches glued over holes in the fabric of wings and fuselage. A crop-dusting outfit? Did the French have crop-dusting outfits? Then he realized that those things in front of the cockpits were machine guns. Air-cooled machine guns rigged to shoot through the propeller. And those odd, oval-shaped tail assemblies . . .

Some kind of museum?

"That is strange aeroplane you have," the mustached soldier said. His accent was as thick as the grass on the field. "One like it I have not seen."

Farman hadn't known that either of them spoke English. "I'll need to make some phone calls," he said, thinking of the ambassador in Paris. A mechanic was working on one of the planes they passed; he was standing on a wooden packing crate, tinkering with the engine.

A movie outfit, doing a period flick? But he didn't see any cameras.

Another biplane taxied in from the field—a Nieuport, like the others. Its engine racketed like a lawnmower. It joggled and bounced in the chuckholes. There were a lot of chuckholes in the mud at the pavement's fringe. The

plane came up on the pavement and the engine cut out.
As the propeller turned around to a spasmodic stop,
Farman realized that not just the propeller but the whole
engine had been spinning. What kind of crazy way to
build airplanes was that?

The Nieuport's pilot climbed up out of the cockpit and
dropped to the ground. "Guns jammed again!" he yelled
loudly, hellishly mad. He flung a small hammer on the
ground at his feet.

Three men came out of the hangar carrying packing
crates. They set them down around the Nieuport's nose,
got up on them, and started working on the guns. The flier
pulled off his scarf and draped it over the cockpit's side.
He turned away, spoke a few French words over his
shoulder to the mechanics, and walked off.

"Monsieur Blake!" the big soldier hailed. When the flier
didn't seem to hear, the soldier ran to him, caught his
shoulder. "Monsieur Blake. A countryman." The soldier
beside Farman pointed to the flag on Farman's sleeve.

Blake came over, stuffing a goggled cloth helmet into a
pocket of his heavy overcoat as he approached. His hand
was out in welcome.

"This one has teach all my *Anglais* to me," the big
trooper grinned. "Is good, *non?*"

Farman scarcely heard him. All his attention was on
this American. "Harry Blake," the man introduced himself. " 'Fraid I won't be able to hear you too good for a
while." He swung a glance at his Nieuport's motor and
raised hands to his ears to signify deafness. He was
young—not more than twenty-two or -three—but he had
the mature poise of a man much older. "I'm a Lafayette
with this outfit. From Springfield, Illinois. You?"

Farman accepted the hand in numb silence. By calling
himself a Lafayette, the flier had obliterated Farman's last

incredulous doubt. It wasn't possible—not real. Things like this didn't happen.

"Hey, you don't look so good," Blake said, grabbing his arm with a strong hand.

"I'll be all right," Farman said, but he wasn't really sure.

"Come on." Blake steered Farman into the passageway between two of the hangars. "We've got what you need back here."

The troopers came after them. "Monsieur Blake. This man has only now arrived. He has not reported."

Blake waved them away. "I haven't either. We'll report later. Can't you see when a man's breathed too much oil?"

The soldiers turned back. Blake's hand steered Farman onward. Puddles slopped under Blake's boots.

Behind the hangars, the path split in two directions. One way led to a latrine whose door swung loose in the breeze. The other led to a shack huddled up to the back of a hangar. It was hard to guess which path was more frequently used. Blake paused at the parting of the ways. "Think you can make it?"

"I'm all right." He wasn't, really. It takes more than a deep breath and a knuckling of the eyes to adjust a man to having lost six and a half decades. Between books about aerial combat he'd devoured as a kid—two wars and all those brushfire skirmishes—he'd read some Heinlein and Asimov. If it wasn't for that, he'd have had nothing to hang on to. It was like a kick in the belly.

"I'll be all right," he said.

"You're sure? You breathe castor oil a few hours a day and it doesn't do a man's constitution much good. Nothin' to be embarrassed about."

Every now and then, Farman had heard castor oil mentioned, mostly in jokes, but he'd never been sure what it did to a man. Now he remembered it had been used in aircraft engines of this time. Suddenly, he understood all. "That's one problem I don't have."

Blake laughed. "It's a problem we all have." He pushed open the shack's door. Farman went inside at his nod. Blake followed. "Onree!" Blake called out. "Two double brandies."

A round little baldpated Frenchman got up from a stool behind the cloth-draped trestle that served as a bar. He poured two glasses almost full of something dark. Blake picked up one in each hand. "How many for you?"

Whatever it was, it looked evil. "One," Farman said, "for a start." Either this youngster was showing off— which didn't seem likely—or it wasn't as deadly as it looked. "A double, that is."

Blake led the way to a table in the far corner, next to a window. It was a plain wood table, stained and scarred. Farman set his glass down and took a chair before he tried a small taste. It was like a trickle of fire all the way down. He looked at the glass as if it had fangs. "What is this stuff?"

Blake had sampled from each glass on the way to the table, to keep them from spilling. Now he was almost halfway through one of them and the other was close to his hand. "Blackberry brandy," he said with a rueful grin. "It's the only cure we've found. Would you rather have the disease?"

Flight medicine, Farman thought, had a long way to go. He put his glass carefully aside. "My plane doesn't use that kind of oil."

Blake was on him right away. "Something new? I thought they'd tried everything."

"It's a different kind of engine," Farman said. He had to do something with his hands. He took a sip of the brandy, choked, regretted it.

"How long you been flying?" Blake asked.

"Ten, twelve years."

Blake had been about to finish his first glass. He set it down untouched, looked straight at Farman. Slowly, a grin came. "All right. A joke's a joke. You going to be flying with us?"

"Maybe. I don't know," Farman said, holding his brandy glass in both hands, perfectly steady—and all the time, deep inside, the small trapped being that was himself screamed silently, *What's happened to me? What's happened?*

It had been a tricky mission, but he'd flown a lot of tricky ones. Ostensibly, he'd been taking part in a systems-test/training exercise off the northwest coast of Africa. High-altitude Mach 4 aircraft, their internal equipment assisted by the tracking and computer equipment on converted aircraft carriers, were attempting to intercept simulated ballistic warheads making re-entry into the atmosphere. He'd lifted from the deck of the airplane tender *Eagle* in the western Mediterranean. Half an hour later he was circling at Big Ten—one-zero-zero thousand feet—on-station north of the Canary Islands when the signal came that sent him on his true mission.

A guidance system had gone wrong at the Cape, said the talker aboard the *Iwo Jima*, and the range-safety system had failed. The misdirected warhead was arching over the Atlantic, farther and higher than programmed. Instead of splashing in the Atlantic, its projected impact-point was deep in the Sahara. It carried only a concrete block, not thermonuclear weaponry, but diplomatic relations with France—which still maintained military bases in this land it had once governed—were troublesome. Standing orders for such an eventuality were that, as a good-faith demonstration, an attempt should be made to intercept it.

Operation Skeetshoot's master computer said Farman's *Pika-Don* was the only plane able to make the interception. No other plane was in the right position. No other plane had enough altitude or fuel load. No other plane had such an advantageous direction of flight at that moment. Farman sent *Pika-Don* streaking toward interception point at full thrust.

As planned.

Nothing had really gone wrong at the Cape. It was a pretext. Washington knew the French were about to test a new-model nuclear bomb. They would explode it above the atmosphere, in the Van Allen belt; the rocket would be launched from their main testing site, the Saharan oasis of Reggan; they would select the moment of launch to coincide with the arrival of a solar proton storm, when subnuclear particles from the storm would blend with the bomb's fission products, rendering surveillance by other nations more difficult and the findings less certain.

The proton storm had been already on its way when Farman left the *Eagle*'s deck. It was being tracked, not only by American installations around the world, but by French stations also. Code message traffic was high between New Caledonia and Reggan. The time of the storm's arrival was known to within five seconds.

Farman hadn't paid much attention to why Washington wanted to snoop the test; the French were, after all, still allies in spite of the frictions between Paris and Washington. Asking questions like that wasn't Farman's job; he was just the airplane driver. But they'd told him anyway, when they gave him the mission. Something about Washington wanting to have up-to-date knowledge of France's independent nuclear capability. Such information was needed, they said, for accurate judgment of how dependent France might still be on America's ability to wage modern war. To Farman, the explanation didn't mean much; he didn't understand much about international politics.

But a warhead dropping into the atmosphere, sheathed in the meteor-flame of its fall—*that* he could understand. And a multi-megaton fireball a hundred miles up, blazing like the sun brought suddenly too close—that, too, he could understand. And a Mach 4 airplane riding her shock-wave across the sky, himself inside watching instruments and flight-path guide scopes, and his thumb on the button that would launch the Lance rockets sheathed against her belly. Those were things he understood. They were his job.

Nor did the mission call for him to do more than that. All that was really necessary was to have *Pika-Don* somewhere in the sky above Reggan when the French bomb went off. *Pika-Don* would do everything else, automatically.

All the planes in Operation Skeetshoot were equipped the same as *Pika-Don*. All of them carried elaborate flight recorders; and because they were fitted to intercept thermonuclear warheads, and their own Lance rockets had sub-kiloton fission tips, those recorders included all the instruments needed to monitor a nuclear explosion— even a unit to measure the still not fully understood magnetohydrodynamic disturbances that played inside a nuclear fireball. (And, it was known from previous tests, there was something unusual about the magnetic fields of French bombs.)

Nor would there be much risk if *Pika-Don* were forced down where French nosypokes could get a look at it. All *Pika-Don* carried was standard equipment—equipment the French already knew about, in configurations and for purposes they also understood. There would be nothing

the French could find to support a charge of deliberate
snooping, no matter how much they might suspect. Not
that the possibility was large; the explosion, after all,
would be out in space. There'd be no blast effects,
certainly, and very little radiation. Enough to tickle the
instruments, was all.

And already the hot line between Washington and
Paris would be explaining why an American plane was
intruding on French-controlled airspace. Everything had
been planned.

Farman watched his instruments, his flight-path guide
scopes, his radar. *Pika-Don* slashed the thin air so fast she
drew blood. She was up to one-three-zero thousand now;
rocket launch point lay five thousand higher, two hundred
miles ahead. Reggan moved onto the edge of the inertial-
guide map-position scope, ahead and off to the south. The
projected trajectory of the warhead was a red line
striking downward on the foreview guide scope. An
X-slash marked Skeetshoot Control's computed interception point.

Something flared on the radar near Reggan. It rose,
slowly for a moment, then asymptotically faster and
faster, shining on the radar screen like a bright, fierce
jewel. The French rocket. Farman's breath caught as he
watched it. The thing was going up. The test was on.

It rose, was level with him, then higher. Suddenly, it
quivered like a water drop, and suddenly it was gone from
the screen in an expanding black blindness like a hole in
the universe; and simultaneously the cockpit was full of
unendurable white light. The sky was flaming, so bright
Farman couldn't look at it, didn't dare. He had just time
enough to think, terrified, *Not in the Van Allen belt!* and
then *Pika-Don* was spinning, spinning, spinning like a
spindle—light flashing into the cockpit, then blackness,
brightness, then blackness again, repeating and repeating

faster and faster and faster until light and darkness merged to a flickering brilliance that dazzled not only the eyes but the whole brain. Farman battled the controls, but it was like fighting the Almighty's wrath. The flickering blaze went on and on.

And slowed. Stopped, like the last frame of film in a halted movie projector, and it was only daylight again, and *Pika-Don*'s disabled pilot circuit had cut in. She was flying level, northwestward if the compass could be trusted, and if the sun's position could be trusted, the afternoon was more than half gone. Farman was sure that much time had not passed.

The map scope confirmed the compass. So did the airspace radar view. The controls felt all right now, and *Pika-Don* seemed to fly without difficulty. He turned straight north toward the Mediterranean and came out above it not far from Oran. He curved west then, toward the spot where he'd left the *Eagle*. He watched the foreview guide scope for the *Eagle*'s homing beacon. It didn't show up. He spoke on the radio, got no answer. Equipment damage?

He took *Pika-Don* down to fifty thousand. He used the telescope-view scope on the ships his radar picked out. None was the *Eagle*; old freighters, mostly, and two small warships of a type he'd thought wasn't used any more except by the Peruvian Navy.

His orders said, if he couldn't find his base ship, go to Frankfurt. The big base there could take him. He turned *Pika-Don* northwestward. He crossed the French coast. Overcast covered the land. It shouldn't have been there. Fuel began to run low. It was going into the engines faster than the distance to Frankfurt was narrowing. He tried to cut fuel consumption, but he couldn't cut it enough. He had no choice but to put down in France.

"Look, Mister, either you've got orders to fly with us, or you don't," Blake said. "What outfit are you with?"

It was restricted information, but Farman didn't think it mattered much. "The CIA, I think."

He might as well have said the Seventh Cavalry with General Custer. "Where's your base?" Blake asked.

Farman took another swallow of brandy. He needed it, even if not for the reason Blake thought. It wasn't so bad, this time. He tried to think of a way to explain the thing that had happened to him. "Did you ever read *The Time Machine*?" he asked.

"What's that? A book about clocks?"

"It's a story by H. G. Wells."

"Who's H. G. Wells?"

He wasn't going to make much explanation by invoking H. G. Wells. "It's about a man who . . . who builds a machine that moves through time the way an airplane moves in the air."

"If you're having fun with me, you're doing it good," Blake said.

Farman tried again. "Think of a building—a tall building, with elevators in it. And suppose you don't know about elevators—can't even imagine how they work. And suppose you were on the ground floor, and suppose I came up and told you I was from the twentieth floor."

"I'd say that's doing a lot of supposing," Blake said.

"But you get the idea?"

"Maybe. Maybe not."

"All right. Now imagine that the ground floor is now. Today. And the basement is yesterday. And the second floor is tomorrow, and the third floor is the day after tomorrow, and so on."

"It's a way of thinking about things," Blake said.

Give thanks the elevator had been invented. "Take it one step more, now. Suppose you're on the ground floor, and someone comes down from the twentieth floor."

"He'd of come from somewhere the other side of next week," Blake said.

"That's the idea," Farman said. He took more of the brandy. "What if I told you I . . . just fell down the elevator shaft from sixty-some years up?"

Blake appeared to consider while he started on his second glass. He permitted himself a smile and a chuckle. "I'd say a man's got to be a bit crazy if he wants to fly in this war, and if you want to fight Huns you've come to the right place."

He didn't believe. Well, you couldn't expect him to. "I was born in nineteen fifty-three," Farman told him. "I'm thirty-two years old. My father was born in nineteen twenty. Right now, it's nineteen . . . seventeen?"

"Nineteen *eighteen*," Blake said. "June tenth. Have another brandy."

Farman discovered his glass was empty. He didn't remember emptying it. Shakily, he stood up. "I think I'd better talk to your commanding officer."

Blake waved him back to his chair. "Might as well have another brandy. He hasn't come back yet. My guns jammed and I couldn't get them unjammed, so I came home early. He'll be back when he runs out of bullets or fuel, one or the other."

His back was to the door, so he had to twist around while still talking, to see who came in. The small, razor-mustached man draped his overcoat on a chair and accepted the brandy the barman had poured without having to be asked. "Today, M'sieu Blake, it was a small bit of both." His English had only a flavor of accent. "On coming back, I find I am left with one bullet."

"How was the hunting?"

The Frenchman gave a shrug that was as much a part of France as the Eiffel Tower. "Ah, that man has the lives of a cat, the hide of an old bull elephant, and the skills of a magician."

"Keyserling?" Blake asked.

The newcomer took a chair at the table. "Who else? I have him in my sights. I shoot, and he is gone. It would be a shame to kill this man—he flies superbly!—and I would love to do it very much." He smiled and sipped his brandy.

"This is our CO," Blake said. "Philippe Deveraux. Thirty-three confirmed kills and maybe a dozen not confirmed. The only man on this part of the front with more is Keyserling." He turned to Farman. "I don't think I got your name."

Farman gave it. "He's just over from the States," Blake said. "And he's been funning me with the craziest story you ever heard."

Farman didn't bother to protest. In similar shoes, he'd be just as skeptical. "This Keyserling," he said. "That's Bruno Keyserling?"

He'd read about Keyserling; next to Richthofen, Bruno Keyserling had been the most hated, feared, and respected man in the German air force.

"That's him," Blake said. "There's not a one of us that wouldn't like to get him in our sights." He set his empty glass down hard. "But it won't happen that way. He's gotten better men than us. Sooner or later, he'll get us all."

Deveraux had been delicately sipping his drink. Now he set it down. "We shall talk of it later, M'sieu Blake," he said firmly. He addressed Farman. "You have been waiting for me?"

"Yes. I . . ." Suddenly, he realized he didn't know what to say.

"Don't give him the same you gave me," Blake warned. "Now it's business."

"You are a pilot, M'sieu Farman?" Deveraux asked.

Farman nodded. "And I've got a plane that can fly faster and climb higher than anything you've got. I'd like a try at this Keyserling."

"That could possibly be arranged. But I should warn you, M'sieu . . . Farman, did you say?"

"Howard Farman."

"I should warn you, the man is a genius. He has done things his aeroplane should not be possible to do. He has shot down forty-six, perhaps more. Once three in a day. Once two in five minutes. It has been said the man came from nowhere—that he is one of the gods from the *Nibelungenlied*, come to battle for his fatherland. He . . ."

"You might say I'm from nowhere, too," Farman said. "Me and my plane."

When Deveraux had finished his brandy and when Blake had downed his fourth, they went out in front of the hangars again. Farman wanted them to see *Pika-Don*. *Pika-Don* would be at least sixty years ahead of any plane they'd ever seen.

Her skids had cut into the turf like knives. Blake and Deveraux examined her from end to end. They walked around her, their boot tips whipping the grass. "Don't touch anything," Farman told them. "Even a scratch in the wrong place could wreck her." He didn't add that the rockets concealed under her belly could vaporize everything within a hundred yards. The false-skin strips that sealed them from the slipstream were supposed to be tamper-proof, but just to be safe Farman placed himself where they would have to go past him to investigate *Pika-Don*'s underside.

Pika-Don was eighty-nine feet long. Her shark-fin wings spanned less than twenty-five. She was like a needle dart, sleek and shiny and razor-sharp on the leading edge of her wings. Her fuselage was oddly flat-bodied, like a cobra's hood. Her airscoops were like tunnels.

Blake crouched down to examine the gear that retracted the skids. Farman moved close, ready to interrupt if Blake started to fool with the rockets. Instead, Blake discovered the vertical thrust vents and lay down to peer up into them. Deveraux put his head inside one of the tail pipes. It was big enough to crawl into. Slowly, Blake rolled out from under and got to his feet again.

"Do you believe me now?" Farman asked.

"Mister," Blake said, looking at him straight, "I don't know what this thing is, and I don't know how you got it here. But don't try to tell me it flies."

"How do you think I got it here?" Farman demanded. "I'll show you. I'll . . ." He stopped. He'd forgotten he was out of fuel. "Ask your ground crews. They saw me bring her down."

Blake shook his head, fist on hips. "I know an aeroplane when I see one. This thing can't possibly fly."

Deveraux tramped toward them from the tail. "This is indeed the strangest zeppelin I have ever been shown, M'sieu. But obviously, a zeppelin so small—so obviously heavy . . . it can hardly be useful, M'sieu."

"I tell you, this is a *plane*. An *air*plane. It's faster than anything else in the air."

"But it has no wings, M'sieu. No propeller. It does not even have wheels on the undercarriage. How can such a thing as this gain airspeed if it has no wheels?"

Farman was speechless with exasperation. Couldn't they see? Wasn't it obvious?'

"And why does it have so strong the scent of paraffin?"
Deveraux asked.

A Nieuport buzzed over the hangars in a sudden burst
of sound. It barrel-rolled twice, turned left, then right,
then came down onto the grass. Its engine puttered. Its
wires sang in the wind. It taxied across the field toward
them.

"That'll be Mermier," Blake said. "He got one."

Two more planes followed. They did no acrobatics—
merely turned into the wind and set down. They bounced
over the turf toward the hangars. One had lost part of its
upper wing. Shreds of cloth flickered in the breeze.

Blake and Deveraux still watched the sky beyond the
hangars, but no more planes came. Blake's hand clapped
Deveraux's shoulder. "Maybe they landed somewhere
else."

Deveraux shrugged. "And perhaps they did not live
that long. Come. We shall find out."

They walked to the other end of the flight line where
the three planes straggled up on the hardstand. Deveraux
hurried ahead and Mermier and then the other two pilots
climbed out of their cockpits. They talked in French, with
many gestures. Farman recognized a few of the gestures
—the universal language of air combat—but others were
strange or ambiguous. Abruptly, Deveraux turned away,
his face wearing the look of pain nobly borne.

"They won't come back," Blake told Farman quietly.
"They were seen going down. Burning." His fist struck
the hangar's wall. "Keyserling got Michot. He was the
only one of us that had a hope of getting him."

Deveraux came back. His face wore a tight, controlled
smile. "M'sieu Farman," he said. "I must ask to be shown
the abilities of your machine."

"I'll need five hundred gallons of kerosene," Farman said. That would be enough for a lift-off, a quick crack through the barrier, and a landing. Ten minutes in the air, if he didn't drive her faster than Mach 1.4. Enough to show them something of the things *Pika-Don* could do.

Devereaux frowned, touched his mustache, "Kerosene?"

"Paraffin," Blake said. "Lamp oil." He turned to Farman. "They call it paraffin over here. But five hundred gallons—are you nuts? There isn't an aeroplane flying that needs that much lubricating. Shucks, this whole *escadrille* doesn't use that much *gas* in a week. Besides, it's no good as a lubricant—if it was, you think we'd be using the stuff we do?"

"It's not a lubricant," Farman said. "She burns it. It's fuel. And she burns it fast. She delivers a lot of thrust."

"But . . . five hundred gallons!"

"I'll need that much just for a demonstration flight." He looked straight and firmly into Blake's incredulous eyes and decided not to add that, fully loaded, *Pika-Don* took fifty thousand gallons.

Deveraux smoothed his mustache. "In liters, that is how much?"

"You're going to let him . . . ?"

"M'sieu Blake, do you believe this man a fraud?"

Challenged like that, Blake did not back down. "I think he's funning us. He says he'll show us an aeroplane, and he showed us that . . . that thing over there. And when you want to see how it flies, he says it's out of fuel and asks for kerosene—*kerosene* of all things! Enough to go swimming in! Even if that's what she burns, he doesn't need anywhere near that much. And who ever heard of flying an aeroplane with lamp oil?"

Farman took Blake's arm, joggled it, made him turn. "I know," he said. "I'm telling you things it's hard to believe.

In your shoes, I wouldn't believe me, either. All right. But let me have a chance to show you. I want to fight the Germans as much as you do." In his thoughts was the picture of a whole *jagdstaffel* of Albatrosses being engulfed by the fireball of one of *Pika-Don*'s rockets. They'd never even see him coming, he'd come at them so fast; even if they saw him, they wouldn't have a chance. Sitting ducks. Fish in a barrel.

"Mister," Blake said, "I don't know what you want all that kerosene for, but I'm sure of one thing—you don't need it to fly. Because if I was ever sure of anything, I know that thing can't fly."

"M'sieu Blake," Deveraux said, moving in front of the American. "This man may perhaps be mistaken, but I do not think he lies. He has a faith in himself. We have need of such men in this war. If he cannot use the paraffin when we have obtained it for him, it will be given to the chef for his stoves. We shall have lost nothing. But we must let him prove his abilities, if he can, for if there is some portion of truth in his claims, why, it is possible that we have before us the man and the machine that shall hurl Bruno Keyserling from the sky."

Blake gave way grudgingly. "If you're funning us, watch out."

"You'll see," Farman promised, grim. And to Deveraux: "Make it a high-grade kerosene. The best you can get." A jet engine could burn kerosene if it had to, but kerosene wasn't a perfect jet fuel any more than wood alcohol could make good martinis. Kerosene was just the nearest thing to jet fuel he could hope to find in 1918. "And we'll have to put it through some kind of filters."

"M'sieu," Deveraux said. "There is only one kind of paraffin. Either it is paraffin, or it is not."

Two days later, while they were waiting for the kerosene to come, Blake took him up in a Caudron two-seater to show him the landmarks. It was a clear day, with only a little dust haze in the direction of the front. Farman didn't think much of learning the landmarks—*Pika-Don*'s map scope was a lot more accurate than any amount of eyeball knowledge. But the scope wouldn't show him the front-line trenches twisting across the landscape, or the location of the German airfields. It might be useful to know such things. Farman borrowed flying clothes, and they were off.

The Caudron looked like nothing so much as a clumsy box kite, or a paleolithic ancestor of the P-38. Its two racketing engines were suspended between the upper and lower wings, one on either side of the passenger nacelle. The tail empennage was joined to the wings by openwork frames of wire-braced wood that extended back from behind the engines. It had a fragile appearance, but it held together sturdily as it lurched across the field like an uncontrolled baby carriage. Finally, after what seemed an interminable length of bumping and bouncing it lofted into the air at a speed that seemed hardly enough to get a feather airborne. A steady windblast tore at Farman's face. Hastily, he slipped the goggles down over his eyes. The climb to six thousand feet seemed to take years.

Blake didn't turn out of their spiral until they reached altitude, then headed east. The air seemed full of crests and hollows, over which the Caudron rode like a boat on a slow-swelled sea. Now and then, woozily, it swayed. A queasy feeling rooted itself in Farman's midsection, as if his stomach was being kneaded and squeezed.

Airsick? No, it couldn't be that. Anything but that. He was an experienced flier with more than ten thousand hours in the air. He couldn't possibly be airsick now. He swallowed hard and firmly held down.

Blake, in the cockpit behind him, yelled and pointed

over the side. Farman leaned over. The rush of air almost ripped his goggles off. Far below, small as a diorama, the trench systems snaked across a strip of barren ground— two latticework patterns cut into the earth, roughly parallel to each other, jaggedly angular like toothpick structures that had been crushed. Between them, naked earth as horribly pocked as the surface of the moon.

The Caudron had been following a rivercourse. The trenchlines came down from the hills to the south, crossed the river, and continued northward into the hills on that side. Ahead, over the German trenches, black puffs of antiaircraft fire blossomed in spasmodic, irregular patterns. Blake banked the Caudron and turned south, yelling something over his shoulder about the Swiss border. The antiaircraft barrage slacked off.

Recognizing the front would be no problem, Farman decided. He tried to tell Blake, but the slipstream ripped the words away. He twisted around to say it straight. Something snatched at his sleeve.

He looked. Something had gashed the thick fabric, but there was nothing in sight that could have done it. And for some unaccountable reason Blake was heeling the Caudron over into a dive. The horizon tilted crazily, like water sloshing in a bowl. The Caudron's wire rigging snarled nastily.

"Use the gun!" Blake yelled. He jerked an urgent thumb upward.

There was a machine gun on the upper wing, above and just aft of Farman's cockpit, but for a shocked moment Farman didn't grasp what Blake was talking about. Then a dark airplane shape flashed overhead, so close the buzz of its motor could be heard through the noise of the Caudron's own two engines. The goggled, cruel-mouthed face of its pilot turned to look at them. Blake threw the Caudron into a tight turn that jammed Farman deep in his cockpit. Farman lost sight of the German plane, then found it again. It was coming at them.

It was purple—a dark royal purple—with white trim around the edges of wing and tail, and around the engine cowl. Little flashes of light sparked from its nose, and Farman heard something—it sounded like thick raindrops—spattering the upper wing close to the passenger nacelle. Tracer bullets flashed past like quick fireflies.

"Use the gun!" Blake yelled again. They were climbing now. They leveled off, turned. The German plane came after them. "Use the gun!"

He was being shot at. It was appalling. Things like that didn't happen. In a moment, Farman was too busy to think about it. Somehow he got his seat belt off and stood up in the cockpit, back to the wind. He fumbled with the machine gun's unfamiliar grips. He found the trigger before he knew what it was. The gun chattered and bucked in his grasp. He looked all over the sky for the purple airplane. It was nowhere in sight. Blake hurled the Caudron through another violent maneuver that almost threw Farman overboard, and suddenly there were three German planes behind them, high, the one with the white trim in front and the others trailing. The one with the white trim shifted a little to the left, turned inward again. It nosed down, gun muzzles flickering.

Farman swung the machine gun to bear on the German. He pressed the trigger. The gun stuttered and a spray of tracers streamed aft as it caught in the slipstream. They passed under the German, not even close.

Aerial gunnery wasn't a thing Farman had ever had to learn. Combat was done with guidance systems, computers, and target-seeking missiles, not antique .30 caliber popguns. He raised the gun and fired another burst. Still too low, and passing behind the German, who was boring close in, weaving up, sidewise, and down as he

came. The gun didn't have any sights worth mentioning—
no target tracking equipment at all. Farman wrestled with
the clumsy weapon, trying to keep its muzzle pointed at
the German. It should have been easy, but it wasn't. The
German kept dodging. Farman emptied the machine gun
without once touching the other plane. He spent an
eternity dismounting the empty magazine and clipping
another into place, all the time holding on one-handed,
while Blake hurled the Caudron through a wild series of
gut-wrenching acrobatics.

A section of the cockpit coaming at Farman's knee
shattered and disappeared in the wind. He got the gun
working again—fired a burst just as the German sidled
behind the Caudron's right rudder. Farman's tracers went
right through. The rudder exploded in a spray of chips
and tatters. The German swung out to the right, gained a
few feet altitude, turned in again and down again. His
guns hurled blazing streaks. Blake sent the Caudron into
a dive, a turn, and a twist that almost somersaulted
Farman out of the plane. Abruptly, then, the German was
gone. Little scraps were still tearing loose from the
rudder, whipped away by the slipstream.

"Where?" Farman shouted, bending down as close to
Blake as he could. He meant, where had the German
gone, but he wasn't up to asking a question that complicated.

"Skedaddled," Blake yelled up at him. "We've got
friends. Look."

Farman looked when Blake aimed his thumb. Five
hundred feet above them five Nieuports cruised in neat
formation. After a moment, the formation leader waggled
his wings and they curved off eastward. Farman looked
down and saw they were far behind the French lines,
headed northwest. They were flying level and smooth—
only the slow, gentle lift and descent of random air

currents, like silence at the end of a storm. He sagged down into his cockpit. "You all right?" Blake asked.

"I think so," Farman said. But suddenly, as the Caudron slipped into a downdraft, he wasn't. His stomach wrenched, and he had time enough only to get his head over the cockpit's side before the first gush of vomit came. He was still there, gripping the splintered coaming with both hands, his stomach squeezing itself like a dry sponge, when Blake circled the airfield and slowly brought the Caudron down to a three-point landing. All Farman could think—distantly, with the part of his brain not concerned with his terrible miseries—was how long it had been since anyone, anywhere in the world, had even thought about making a three-point landing.

He wouldn't admit, even to himself, it had been airsickness. But after a while the horizon stopped wheeling around him and he could stand without needing a hand to steady him. He discovered he was very hungry. Blake went down to the mess hall and came back with a half-loaf of black bread and a dented tin of pâté. They went to the shack behind the hangars. Henri gave Blake a bottle of peasant's wine and two glasses. Blake put them down in the middle of the table and sat down across from Farman. He poured, and they went to work on the bread and pâté.

"He was trying to kill us," Farman said. It just came out of him. It had been there ever since the fight. "He was trying to *kill* us."

Blake cut himself another slice of the bread. He gnawed on the leathery crust. "Sure. And I'd of killed him, given the chance. That's what we're supposed to do—him and us, both. Nothing personal at all. I've got to admit I wasn't expecting him, though. They don't often come this side of the lines. But . . ." He made a rueful grimace. "He's a tough one to outguess."

"He?"

Blake stopped gnawing, frowned. "You know who it was, don't you?"

The idea of knowing an enemy's name after such a brief acquaintance was completely strange to Farman. His mouth made motions, but no words came out.

"Bruno Keyserling," Blake said. "He's the only man with an aeroplane painted that way."

"I'm going to get him," Farman said.

"Easier said than done," Blake said. His mouth turned grim. "You'll have to sharpen up your gunnery quite a bit, if you're going to make good on that."

"I'm going to get him," Farman repeated, knuckles white on the table.

The next day it rained. Thick, wet, gray clouds crouched low to the ground and poured down torrents. All patrols were canceled, and the fliers sat in the shack behind the hangers, drinking and listening to the storm as it pelted the shingles. At first light, when he woke and heard the rain, Farman had borrowed a slicker and gone out to *Pika-Don*. She was all right. He'd left her buttoned up tight, and the rain was doing her no harm.

Blake was still the only man Farman could talk with, except for Deveraux. None of the other pilots had more than a smattering of English. When they left the mess hall after a drab lunch, instead of returning to the drinking shack, Blake led him to one of the hangars. There, in a back corner, were stacked wooden boxes of ammunition and others full of the bent-metal sections of disintegrating-link machine-gun belts. Blake showed Farman how to assemble the links and how to check both the links and the cartridges for manufacturing defects. He handed Farman a gauge into which a properly shaped cartridge should fit perfectly, and they spent the next several hours inspecting cartridges and assembling belts of ammunition. It was tedious work. Each cartridge looked just like the one before it. The imperfections were small.

"Do you always do this yourself?" Farman inspected his grimy hands, his split cuticles. He wasn't accustomed to this kind of work. "Every chance I get," Blake said. "There're enough reasons for a gun to jam without bad ammunition being one of 'em. When you're up there with Keyserling's circus flying rings around you, all you've got are your guns and your engine and your wings, and if any of those go, you go. And it's a long way down."

Farman said nothing for a while. Rain drummed on the roof. Now and then came the clang of tools being used in another part of the hangar. "How come you're here?" he asked finally. "What's in it for you?"

Blake's busy hands paused. He looked at Farman. "Say that again, slower."

"This here's a French squadron. You're an American. What are you doing here?"

Blake snorted—not quite a chuckle. "Fighting Germans."

Farman wondered if Blake was making fun of him. He tried again. "Sure—but why with a bunch of Frenchmen?"

Blake inspected a cartridge, fitted it into the belt. He picked up another. "Didn't care to transfer," he said. "Could have, when they started bringing U.S. squadrons over. But I like the plane I've got. If I transferred, they'd give me a plane the French don't want and the British don't want, because that's all the American squadrons are getting. Well, I don't want 'em, either." He dropped a cartridge in the reject pile.

"I didn't mean that," Farman said. "You joined before America got into the war—right?"

"Came over in 'sixteen."

"All right. That's what I mean. Why help France?" He couldn't understand why an American would do anything to help the personal kingdom of *le grand Charles.* "You weren't involved," he said. "Why?"

Blake went on inspecting cartridges. "Depends what you mean, involved. I figure I am. Everyone is. The Germans started this war. If we can show the world it doesn't pay to start a war, then there won't be any more. I want that. This is going to be the last war the human race will ever have."

Farman went back to inspecting cartridges. "Don't get your hopes too high," he said. It was as near as he could bring himself to telling Blake how doomed his optimism was. The rain made thunder on the roof like the march of armies.

Late in the afternoon, two days later, three lorries sputtered into the supply area behind the hangars. They brought fuel for the escadrille, but also, crowded among the drums of gasoline were twenty hundred-liter barrels of kerosene which were carefully put aside and trucked down to the mess hall's kitchen and then—when the error was discovered—had to be reloaded and trucked back up to the hangars again.

Farman had managed to rig a crude filtration system for the kerosene. The stuff they cooked with was full of junk. He'd scrounged sheets of silk, and enlisted a crew of mechanics to scrub empty petrol drums until their innards gleamed like the insides of dairy cans. He even succeeded in testing the rig with a bucket of kerosene cadged from the kitchens. The process was glacially slow, and the end product neither looked nor smelled any different from the stuff he started with. But when he tried it in one of *Pika-Don*'s engines, the engine had started and—at low r.p.m.—had delivered thrust and functioned as it should until the tank was sucked dry. More important, when he inspected, none of the injectors had fouled.

He started the filtering process, and stayed with it through the night and all the next day. He had a mechanic to help him, but he had no confidence in the mechanic's understanding of how vital fuel quality was to an engine. It was not a thing an airplane mechanic of this time could be expected to know. Deveraux came around once, inspected the raw material and sniffed the filtered product, and went away again, having said nothing.

Once, between missions, Blake came and sat to watch. Farman showed him the sludge the filters had taken out of the kerosene. Blake scowled. "It's still kerosene," he said. "You can't fly an aeroplane on kerosene any more than you can feed it birdseed. I don't know what you really want it for, but don't expect me to believe it's for flying."

Farman shrugged. "I'll take *Pika-Don* up tomorrow morning. You can tell me what you think tomorrow afternoon. Fair enough?"

"Maybe," Blake said.

"You think I'm a cushmaker, don't you?"

"Possible. What's a cushmaker?"

Blake hadn't heard the story. Maybe it hadn't been invented yet. Farman explained it—the ultra shaggy joke about the cushmaker who, obliged by an admiral to demonstrate his specialty, after commandeering a battleship and tons of elaborate equipment, and after arduous technological efforts, finally dropped a white-hot sphere of steel amid the ice floes of the Antarctic Ocean, where it went *cussh.*

Blake went away, then. "I'll say this. If you're pulling a

deal, you're a cool one." He shook his head. "I just don't know about you."

Morning brought high, ragged clouds. They'd make no trouble for the demonstration flight. Farman waited beside *Pika-Don* while Blake took off and slowly climbed to ten thousand feet, circling over the field the whole time. "I think we are ready, M'sieu," Devereaux said, fingering his trim mustache.

Farman turned to his plane. "Better make everybody stand back," he said. Turbine scream wasn't gentle to unprotected ears. He climbed up on the packing crate— pulled himself up *Pika-Don*'s sloped side and dropped into the cockpit. Looking back, he saw the onlookers had retreated about twenty-five feet. He had quite an audience. He grinned. They'd back off a lot farther when he got the engines going.

He got the cockpit hatch down. He checked the seal; it was tight. He went through the pre-ignition cockpit check. He began the engine start-up cycle, felt the momentary vibration and saw the twitch of instruments coming alive. Engine One caught, ragged for an instant, then steady as the tachometer wound around like a clock gone wild. Its scream of power drilled through the cockpit's insulation. Farman started Engine Two, then Engine Three. He brought them up to standby idle. They burned smooth.

Good enough. He didn't have fuel to waste on all the pre-takeoff operations; some were necessary, some not. He did all the necessary ones, turned the jets into the lift vents, and brought them up to full power. By that time, *Pika-Don* was already off the ground. She bobbled momentarily in the light breeze, and rose like a kite on a string. The sprawling fuselage surface prevented him from looking down at the airfield; it didn't matter. They'd be watching, all right—and probably holding shriek-filled ears. He grinned at the trembling instruments in front of him. He wished he could see their eyes, their open mouths. You'd think they'd never seen a plane fly before.

He took *Pika-Don* up to ten thousand feet. Hovering, he tried to find the image of Blake's Nieuport on the airspace view scope. It didn't show. For a worried moment, Farman wondered if something had gone wrong and Blake had gone down. Then the Nieuport flew past him on the left, a little above. It turned to pass in front of him. He could see Blake's goggled face turned toward him.

Even then, there wasn't an image on the radar. Farman swore. Something was wrong with the equipment.

No time to fiddle with the dials now, though. *Pika-Don* was guzzling the kerosene like a drunk on holiday. He converted to lateral flight. As always, it was like the floor dropping out from under him. He moved all three throttles forward, felt the thrust against his back. For a frightened instant, he saw Blake had turned back—was coming straight at him, head-on. He'd warned Blake not to get ahead of him like that. But *Pika-Don* was dropping fast. At speeds less than Mach 0.5 she had the glide capability of a bowling ball. She slashed underneath the Nieuport with a hundred feet to spare. The altimeter began to unwind, faster and faster. The horizon lifted on the forward view scope like a saucer's rim.

He watched the Machmeter. It was edging up. He could feel the drive of the engines, full thrust now, exciting him like they always did, hurling him across the sky. The altimeter steadied, began to rise again. He tipped *Pika-Don*'s prow upward and cracked the barrier in a rocketing fifty-degree climb. Blake's Nieuport was nowhere in sight.

At forty thousand he cut the engines back, leveled off, and started down. He had to search hard for the airfield;

without the map scope he couldn't have found it. It was just another green field in a countryside of green fields. At five thousand feet he converted back to vertical thrust and let *Pika-Don* drop to a landing—quickly for most of the distance to save fuel, with a heavy retarding burst in the last thousand feet. He hovered a moment two hundred feet up, picked out a landing spot, and put down. According to the gauges, less than thirty seconds' fuel was left in the tanks.

He dropped to the ground without waiting for a packing crate to be brought. He stood and looked around in disbelief. There was hardly a man in sight, and none of the escadrille's planes remained on the field. He saw them, finally, small specks flying off eastward. He walked back to the hangars, perplexed. Was that all the impression he'd made? He grabbed the first man he found—a mechanic. "What happened?"

The mechanic grinned and made gestures and gabbled in French. Farman shook him and asked again—or tried to—in pidgin French. All he got was more of the same jabber and some gestures in the general direction of the front lines. "I know they went that way," Farman growled and flung the man away. He stalked back to the shack behind the hangars and asked Henri for a Scotch. He drank it, waited five minutes, and had another. He was deep into his fourth when the men came back.

They trooped into the shack, and Henri set a row of glasses on the counter and went down the line with the brandy bottle. As soon as a glass had been filled, a hand snatched it away. Blake came to Farman's table, a brimful glass in his hand, sat down.

"Howard," he said, "I don't know how that thing of yours works. I don't even know if you can call it an aeroplane. But I've got to admit you got it off the ground, and the only thing I ever saw go past me faster was a bullet. Now, if you'll just tell me one thing . . ."

"Anything you want to know," Farman said, abruptly raised from dejection to smugness.

"How can you fly when you don't have the wind on your face?"

Farman started to laugh, but Blake wasn't even smiling. To him, it wasn't an old joke. He was serious.

With effort, Farman controlled his amusement. "I don't need the wind. In fact, if the window broke, I'd probably be killed. I've got instruments that tell me everything I need to know."

He could see the skeptical expression shaping itself on Blake's face. He started to get up, not quite steady because of the Scotches he'd downed. "Come on. I'll show you the cockpit."

Blake waved him down. "I saw the cockpit. You've got so many things in there you don't have time to look outside. I don't know if I'd call it flying. You might as well be sitting at a desk."

Sometimes, Farman had thought the same thought. But all those instruments were necessary to fly a thing like *Pika-Don*. He wondered if he'd have taken up flying if he'd known it would be like that. "Or maybe a submarine?" he asked, not entirely sarcastic. "The thing is, did I fly circles around you, or didn't I?"

Blake's reply was a rueful shrug. "First, you hung there like a balloon. If I hadn't seen you, I wouldn't believe it. Then all of a sudden you were coming at me like something out of a cannon. I got to admit you had me scared. I never saw anything move like that thing of yours. By the time I got turned around you were out of sight. If we'd been dogfighting, you could of put a string of bullets through me from end to end, and I couldn't of got a shot off."

A shadow intruded onto the table between them. They looked up. "Indeed, M'sieu Farman," Deveraux said, "your machine's speed gives it the ability to attack without the risk of being attacked itself. I will not pretend to understand how it can fly with such small wings, nor how it can rise directly into the air, but I have seen it do these things. That is enough. I must apologize that we could not be here to applaud you when you landed."

So he'd made an impression after all. "Where'd you go? I thought you didn't have any patrols scheduled until this afternoon."

Deveraux pulled out a chair and sat down beside Blake. With delicate care, he placed a half-full wineglass in front of him. "That is true, M'sieu. But we heard the sound of big guns at the front, and our duty is to be in the air at such times, until the matter is clarified, doing such things as will assist our men in the trenches."

"I didn't hear any guns," Farman said. "When I got back here, it was as quiet as a bar mitzvah in Cairo."

He realized almost at once, seeing their faces, that the metaphor had no meaning for them. Well, they hadn't heard of Social Security, either.

"It is curious," Deveraux said. "When we are come to the front, it is as you say—most quiet. The guns have stopped, and we see no aircraft but our own. We search for fifty kilometers along the front. There is no evidence of even small actions. When we come back, I message to commanders at the front, and they tell me there has been no action. Nor have guns in their sectors been made use of—theirs or the Boche—though it is curious . . . some do say that they have heard guns being used in other sectors. And you can see"—he pointed to the window, the clear sky—"it could not have been thunder."

He said it all with the innocent mystification of a small
boy, still not sure of all the things in the universe. Farman
suddenly laughed and Deveraux blinked, startled.

"Sorry." Farman said. "I just realized. It wasn't guns
you heard. It was me."

"You, M'sieu? What jest is this?"

"No joke. What you heard was my plane. It makes a
shock wave in the air, just like an explosion's." He looked
at their faces. "You don't believe me."

Deveraux's wineglass was empty. Blake stood up,
empty brandy glass in hand. He reached for Deveraux's
glass, but the Frenchman put his hand in the way. Blake
went to the bar with only his own glass. Farman nursed
his drink.

"I do not pretend to understand this aeroplane of
yours," Deveraux said. "But now that you have shown its
abilities . . ."

"Some of them," Farman said. They'd only seen an
iceberg tip of what *Pika-Don* could do.

"Yes. But now we have seen," Deveraux said. "I will
agree, it is possible your machine could outmatch Bruno
Keyserling."

"I know she can," Farman said.

"Perhaps," Deveraux said with a small smile, but very
firm. "But I agree—it should be tried. If you will tell us
where to mount the guns on your machine . . ."

"I don't need guns," Farman said. "Don't want them."

"But M'sieu, an aeroplane *must* have guns. Without
guns, it is like a tiger without teeth and claws."

The thought of machine guns stuck on *Pika-Don*'s prow
was a horror. "I've got my own weapons," Farman said.
Blake came back, sat down heavily. His glass slopped a
little on the table. "Machine guns would . . . they'd
destroy her aerodynamic integrity. They'd . . . she probably couldn't even fly with them sticking out in the wind."

"Aerody . . . *what* integrity?" Blake snorted. "What are you talking about?"

Farman leaned forward. "Look. You've seen my plane. All right. Now—you've seen those overlapping strips along her belly, between the ports the skids retract into?"

"I have noticed," Deveraux said.

"There's a rocket under each one of them," Farman said. "Just one of those can wipe out a whole squadron."

"Ah? How many rockets? Eight?"

"Six," Farman said. "How many squadrons have the Germans got in this sector?"

"Two jagdstaffels," Deveraux said. "They are quite enough." He shook his head. "But M'sieu, the men who planned the equipping of your aeroplane did not understand the needs of combat. It is assuming a marksman's skill beyond human abilities to believe that with only six of these rockets you could expect to be effective against enemy aircraft. One must remember, they are not motionless targets, like balloons. It is difficult enough to strike a balloon with rockets—balloons do not move—but to destroy an aeroplane . . . that cannot be done. Often I have expended all my ammunition—hundreds of rounds —without so much as touching my opponent. That you would imagine going into combat with a mere six possibilities of striking your target . . . this is folly. It is not worth the effort."

"They're not just things I shoot off," Farman said. Did he have to explain everything? "In fact, my plane's so fast any weapons system that depends on human senses couldn't possibly work. My rockets find their targets themselves. They are . . ."

He saw the utter disbelief on their faces. "Look," he said, "I've shown you my plane can do everything I told you it could. It flies faster and climbs faster than anything you ever saw. Now, if you'll give me enough fuel to take her up against Keyserling, I'll show you what my rockets can do. They'll wipe him out of the sky like a blob of smoke in a high wind."

"Bruno Keyserling is a very skilled and deadly man," Deveraux said. "A man impossible to kill. We have tried—all of us. He has killed many of our own men, and he will send more of us down in flames before this war ends. I would suggest you be not so confident of yourself and your equipment."

"Just give me enough kerosene for a mission," Farman said. "One mission. Let me worry about the rest of it." He wasn't worried at all. A dogfight between World War I model planes and something from 1985 would be like a wrestling match between a man and a gorilla.

"But M'sieu, you *have* the paraffin," Deveraux said, mildly puzzled. "You have almost two thousand liters."

Farman shook his head. "I burned that. There's just about enough left to fill that glass of yours."

Deveraux looked down at his empty wineglass. "M'sieu, you must be joking."

"No joke," Farman said. "*Pika-Don* flies fast and climbs like a rocket, but you don't get something for nothing—law of conservation of energy, if you know what that is. She drinks fuel like a sewer."

There was a silence—a silence, Farman realized, not only at their own table, but all through the shack. Maybe these fliers understood more English than he thought. Blake downed a large swallow of brandy.

"How much do you need for a mission?" he asked.

"Ten thousand gallons will do for a short one," Farman said. "An hour—hour and a half."

There was another long silence. "M'sieu," Deveraux said at last, "I have wide discretion in the requisition of the usual materials. I am trying to balance in my mind the possible destruction of Bruno Keyserling—which is a thing we all desire—against the difficulty I must expect in explaining my request for so much kitchen fuel. And I remain in doubt you will be able to accomplish as successful as you claim. So I must ask—have I your word of honor as an American that you must have this paraffin to fly your machine?"

"You've got it, on a stack of Bibles."

"The good old USA is alive with con men," Blake said.

"M'sieu Blake," Deveraux said reproachfully, "we must not assume that a man tells lies because he claims ability to do a thing we cannot do ourselves. He is optimistic, yes. But that is a fault of almost all the young men who come to us. If we do not put him to the test, we shall not know if he could do the thing he claims or not."

Blake made a sour twist of his mouth. "All right. But how are you going to explain wanting forty thousand liters of kerosene?"

Deveraux cocked his head to one side, as if listening to a voice no one else could hear. "I think I shall merely tell a part of the truth. That we wish to try a weapon suggested by one of our men, a weapon which makes use of paraffin."

"Such as?" Blake asked.

"If they want details," Farman said, leaning forward, "tell them you're putting it in old winebottles and cramming a rag in the neck. And before you drop the bottle on the Germans you set fire to the rag. The bottle breaks when it hits, and spills burning kerosene over everything."

Blake and Deveraux looked at each other. Delight animated their faces. "Now that's something I think might work," Blake said, rubbing his jaw. "Why didn't somebody think of it before?"

It was the first time Farman had heard him enthusiastic

about something. This, at least, was a weapon they could understand. "It might work," he said. "But gasoline does it better. It's called a Molotov cocktail." ·

"M'sieu Farman," Deveraux said, "I think we shall try that, also." He stood up, wineglass in hand. "Henri!" he called. "More wine!"

Early that afternoon, two men came to the airfield fresh from training school. Boys, really; neither could have been more than seventeen. They were eager to get into the war—looked disconsolate as they came away from reporting to Deveraux. "They'll have to spend a day or two learning their way around," Blake said, a twisty smile curling his mouth. "Some guys just can't wait to get killed."

Their Nieuports were straight from the factory, new as pennies. The smell of dope and varnish surrounded them like an aura. Blake worked his way around them, a point-by-point inspection. The new men would be assigned to his flight. He peered intently at struts and wires and fabric surfaces. "Good aeroplanes," he said finally. Then it was time for him to go out on patrol. Three other men went with him. Farman watched them take off. They disappeared eastward. He went back and saw about readying his jerrybuilt filtration plant for the job of turning ten thousand gallons of cooking oil into aviation fuel.

At first light next morning, the new men stood beside their planes and watched the escadrille fly out on dawn patrol. They looked like children not invited to play. Farman went and checked *Pika-Don*; there was sign of a gummy deposit in her tailpipes, but a close inspection of her compressor blades showed they were clean, and none of the fuel injectors was fouled. He buttoned her up again and headed for the drinking shack. Until he got a shipment of kerosene, he'd have nothing to do.

The escadrille came back three hours later. If there'd been any Germans in the sky that morning, they'd made themselves hard to find. There'd been no action. Six planes refueled at once and went out again. Deveraux took the new men out on an orientation flight. In the afternoon, Blake and another pilot took the new men out for a mock dogfight. When they came back, Farman was waiting at the edge of the field; he had an idea he felt foolish for not having thought of sooner—to make a start on the long kerosene-upgrading job by borrowing a barrel or two of the raw material from the mess hall. He needed Blake to translate and haggle for him.

As Blake taxied up onto the hardstand, Farman saw the tattered fabric fluttering from the right upper wing. He ran over as Blake cut the motor. "Hey! You've been in a fight!"

Blake dropped down from the cockpit. He stripped off helmet and goggles and gloves. Farman repeated his question. Blake grinned and pointed to his ears and shook his head. Farman pointed at the shredded wing.

"Yeah. I've been in a fight," Blake said, his voice loud as if he was trying to talk through the noise his motor had made.

Farman looked out at the other planes taxiing in from the field. "They're all right," Blake said. "We jumped a Brandenburg—what he was doing way off there behind the lines, don't ask me. I got the observer interested in me"—he nodded at the damaged wing—"and Jacques moved in and put a few in the engine. Simple enough."

The other planes of the flight came up on the hard-stand, and the mechanics moved in to turn them around and chock the wheels. The pilots climbed out, and the new men crowded around the other veteran—Jacques, Farman assumed. They pumped his arm and slapped his back and jabbered jubilantly. Jacques managed to break free of them long enough to reach Blake. He grabbed both Blake's arms and spoke with a warm grin. Blake looked a little embarrassed by the attention and managed, finally, to shrug off Jacques' hands without offending. By then the new men had closed in again. A rapid four-way conversation broke out.

Blake got loose again after a minute. "They never saw an aeroplane shot down before." He grinned. "Wasn't much of a shoot-down, really. Jacques put a few in the engine, and it just sort of went into a glide." He nodded at the three men; they were still talking energetically. "I guess they liked the show, even if they don't understand some of it. They're wanting to know why we didn't go on shooting after Jacques got the engine."

It sounded like a reasonable thing to ask. "Well, why didn't you?" He remembered to speak loud.

Blake shrugged. "Why kill 'em? There's enough people getting killed. They were out of the war as soon as their propeller stopped."

"Well, yes. Sure. But . . ."

"Oh, we made sure they landed close to a convoy on the road, so they'd be captured all right," Blake said. "Didn't want a pair of Huns running loose behind the lines."

"But they were Germans. The enemy."

Blake punched a finger into Farman's ribs. "Once Jacques got their engine, they were just a couple of poor guys in an aeroplane that couldn't fly any more. We got no fight with guys like that. It's the man they worked for we're against. The Kaiser. Besides, that guy in the rear cockpit still had a lot of bullets in his machine gun, and he was sort of mad at us. I figure we were smart to keep our distance."

The new men had a few more training flights the next day, and the day after that they went out with the dawn patrol. The patrol met a flight of German machines led by Keyserling's white-trimmed purple Albatross. It was a fast, cruel scrap. Only one of the new men came back.

"We shouldn't of put 'em on service so quick," Blake said, nodding across the shack toward where the survivor was slowly drinking himself into numbness; he'd been in shock ever since he climbed out of his cockpit. "But we've got to have men. It takes three months to train a man enough so he's got a chance in the air—and Keyserling and his circus kill 'em in five minutes. Like swatting a fly." He picked up his brandy and downed it whole.

Deveraux came and put a hand on Blake's shoulder. "It is true," he said. "One might wish we did not so desperately need men to fight. But we fight a war to preserve civilization, and for that it is necessary that some good men die. And so we have lost one man today. And one other machine is damaged. Do not forget, Keyserling has lost two men in this morning's battle, and three of his aeroplanes will need considerable work before they fly again. We have done well, this day."

"Yeah. Sure. But he was just a kid," Blake said. His open hand banged on the table. Glasses rattled. "A poor, dumb kid. As green as—"

"To keep a civilization is worth a few lives, M'sieu Blake." Deveraux squeezed Blake's shoulder, held the grip a moment, let his hand slip away. He moved off to talk with the men at another table.

"Civilization," Blake muttered.

"Stick around," Farman said. If he lived long enough, Blake would know of Dachau, Bataan, Hiroshima, 'Nam, and the bloody mess France herself would make of her African colonies. And lots more.

"You haven't seen anything yet," Farman said.

The kerosene began to come two days later. It came spasmodically, in odd-sized lots: one day a demijohn arrived; the next, half a lorry load. Kerosene, to these people, was not a strategically vital petrochemical; it was a fluid used in lamps and stoves. It couldn't just be commanded up from the nearest supply dump in anything like the quantities a supersonic jet had to have. Genghis Khan's army might have been similarly inept at meeting a sudden, inexplicable demand for a few thousand pounds of gunpowder.

June became July. The summer sun burned warm. There was talk of heavy fighting to the north, in a place called Bois de Belleau. Farman worked at the makeshift filters day after day. The smell of warm kerosene was a weight in his lungs, an ache in his brain. Some evenings, he was too sickened to eat.

The weeks blended into each other. He didn't have much idle time; there was always more kerosene to be poured into the system, or a filter to be changed and the clogged filter to be scraped and scrubbed and carefully examined for flaws before being used again. After a while, he stopped looking up when he heard the sound of airplane motors.

But in that time he saw airplanes lose power as they left the ground, stall, and nose stiffly into the turf. Their wings snapped like jackstraws. He saw a tattered plane coming back from a dogfight; it fell apart over the field and its pilot died in the wreck. He saw a man bring his plane down, taxi off the field, and die from loss of blood with the engine still puttering. And there were many times when he saw men watch the sky, searching for planes that would not come back, ever.

Some nights, he heard the big guns thunder at the front, like a grumbling storm just beyond the horizon. Muzzle flash and shellburst blazed in the sky.

Several days came when no new loads of kerosene arrived. He used that time to learn what he could about the Germans—their tactics, their formations, the capabilities of their planes. Not much of the information was useful—he'd expected that; matched against *Pika-Don*, they'd be almost motionless targets. But with only ten thousand gallons to fly on, it would be a good idea to know where he'd be most likely to find them. He wouldn't have much more time in the air than just enough to lift off, aim and launch rockets, and return to base. He started planning the mission.

"They stay mostly on their own side of the lines," he said to Deveraux. "All right. When I go up, I don't want you to have any planes on that side. I want to be sure any planes I find over there are theirs, not yours. I'll be going too fast to look at 'em close."

"You ask more than is possible, or even wise," Deveraux said. Breeze ruffled grass on the field. The Frenchman's scarf flapped and fluttered. "It is necessary always to have patrols in all sectors to protect our reconnaissance aeroplanes. If we do not patrol, the reconnaissance aeroplanes would be attacked. They could not do their missions. Perhaps it would be possible to remove patrols from one sector for a few hours—one in which none of our observation missions will be flying. Is not that as much as you shall need?"

"Not quite," Farman said. "I don't think you've thought it all the way through. You cover the front between the Swiss border and the Vosges Mountains. Right?"

"There are several escadrilles with which we share that duty."

"Yeah. Well, that's not important except they'll have to be warned off, too. What I'm asking now is, how many miles of front are you covering? Fifty? Seventy-five?"

"It is fifty kilometers," Deveraux said.

"All right. I'll be flying at about Mach 2. At that speed, I can cover that much distance in three minutes. It takes me twenty miles just to get turned around. I can patrol the whole front, all by myself. You don't need to have anybody else out there."

Deveraux's face wore a scowlish mask. "So fast? I must assume you do not exaggerate, M'sieu."

"At sixty thousand feet, I could do it twice that fast," Farman said. "But I'm going to cruise at forty. Air's too thick for full power flying that low down. I'd burn like a meteor."

"Of course, M'sieu."

Farman couldn't be sure if Deveraux believed him or not.

"But I must say, it would seem you have not considered all the necessities," the Frenchman went on. "Even if you are able to patrol all the sectors, that would be true only should you not find a Boche patrol. Then you would move to attack it, and *voilà*, you would be engaged in combat, M'sieu. You would cease to patrol. And it is not uncommon for the Boche to have four or five flights in the air at one time. Who would be protecting our observation missions while you are fighting?"

"I don't even want any observation flights on that side of the lines while I'm flying," Farman said. "Because I'm going to wipe that sky clean like a blackboard. If you have observation planes over there, they might get it, too. So you don't need to have any patrols out to protect 'em. Anyway, it won't take me more than five minutes from the time I've spotted a flight until I've launched rockets, and then I'll be free to go back on patrol. That's not much more than if I'd took time out for a smoke."

They heard, then, very faint but growing, the sound of aircraft motors. Deveraux turned to search the eastward sky for the approaching planes. "And have you thought,

M'sieu, what the Boche would be doing while you are shooting these rockets of yours? Bruno Keyserling and his men are aviators of consummate skill. They would not fly calmly, doing nothing, while you attack them. And even should your rockets each find a target, that would still be only one of their aeroplanes for each rocket. You have, I believe you said, only six."

"They won't even see me coming, I'll jump 'em so fast," Farman said. "They won't have time to do anything but look surprised. And one of my rockets can . . ." He made a wipe-out gesture. "Look. All I'm asking—keep your planes on this side of the lines for a couple of hours. With only ten thousand gallons, I won't be able to stay out even that long. Am I asking too much? Two hours?"

The returning planes were in sight now. There were three of them, strung out, the one in the rear far behind the other two, losing altitude, regaining it, losing it again. Farman didn't know how many had gone out on that particular patrol—he hadn't been paying much attention to such things—but it was rare for a patrol of only three planes to go out. There would be some empty chairs in the mess, this evening.

The first plane came down to land. Its lower wing was shredded close to the fuselage—loose fabric fluttered like torn flags—and the landing gear wheel on that side wobbled oddly. As it touched down, the whole gear collapsed. The wing dipped—caught the ground—and flung the machine into a tangle of broken struts, tail high in the air. Men ran across the field. Farman caught a glimpse of the pilot's arm, waving for help. A thin black thread of smoke began to rise. A moment later it was a fierce inferno. No one could get near it. There wasn't a sign of the man. The second plane landed and taxied across the grass unheeded.

Deveraux turned to Farman again. "No, M'sieu," he

said. "You do not ask too much. It is we who ask too much of men."

Farman boosted *Pika-Don* from the field while dawn was still a growing light in the east and all the land was gray. She lifted sluggishly; well, the gunk he was feeding her was a poor substitute for her usual diet. He took her to eight thousand feet before converting to lateral flight. She was down to four before she cracked the barrier and down to three and a half before she bottomed out and started to climb. The Machmeter moved past 1.25. He raised *Pika-Don*'s nose and drove her at the sky.

She broke into sunlight at twenty thousand feet. The sun was gold and the air was as clean as clear ice. Somewhere in the darkness below two armies faced each other as they had faced each other for four years. At forty thousand feet he leveled off and began his loiter pattern— a slim-waisted figure eight course, looping first to the south, then to the north—overflying the German lines from the Swiss border to the Vosges Mountains. He watched the airspace view scope for the pips that would be German aircraft.

Almost always, on good flying days, the Germans sent up patrols a few minutes before sunrise, to intercept the reconnaissance planes the French almost always sent over on good flying days. Bruno Keyserling would be leading one of those patrols. Farman watched particularly the area surrounding the German airfield. The Germans would climb quickly to fighting altitude; as soon as their altitude and motion dissociated them from the ground, *Pika-Don*'s radars would pick them out. He watched the scope, followed his loiter pattern, and waited for the German planes to appear.

Two circuits later, he was still up there. The scope showed the shaded contours of the land, but that was all.

Not one German plane—no planes at all, even though the whole escadrille had flown out ahead of him to watch the fight he'd promised. He had fuel enough for six or eight more circuits—it was going faster than he'd counted on—before there'd be only enough to get him back to the field.

And more weeks of filtering kerosene? Not if he could help it. He made two more circuits—still nothing. He put *Pika-Don*'s needle prow downward. If they wouldn't come up and fight, he'd go after them. He checked the German field's position on the map scope. He could fly down straight to the end of its runway, and he had six rockets. One would be enough. Two would destroy it utterly.

He was down below twenty thousand feet when he saw the airplanes. They were flying on a northerly course, as he was, patrolling above the German lines in a Junck's row formation—each plane above, behind, and to the side of the one below it; an upright, diagonal line. A quick glance at the radar scope: not a hint of those planes.

Nuts with the airfield. Not with those planes over there. Flying where they were, using that formation, they had to be Germans. Farman pulled out of this attack dive, immelmanned into a corkscrew turn that would take him back and place him behind their formation. He lost sight of them in that maneuver, but the map scope showed him where they had to be; they didn't have the speed to move far while he was getting into position.

Behind them now, he turned again and drove toward them. Still nothing on the airspace scope, but he knew where they were. He tried the target-tracking radar—the one in the middle of the instrument panel. They didn't show there, either.

But he knew where they were, and in another moment he saw them again. Little black specks, like gnats, only gnats didn't fly in formation. And one rocket anywhere near them . . .

Still they didn't show on the target-tracking scope. It would have to be an eyeball launch, then. He primed the proximity detonators on rockets one and six. There still was no sign that they'd seen him. They didn't even seem to move against the sky.

He launched the rockets at four miles. The distance was a guess—without help from his radars, a guess was all he could do, but the German planes were still only specks. It didn't matter. The rockets were built to heat-seek a target from ten times that distance. He felt the shock as the rockets struck from their sheaths even as he sent *Pika-Don* screaming straight up, engines suddenly at full thrust, and over on her back, and a half-roll, and he was at forty-five thousand feet. Rockets one and six sketched their ionized tracks on the airspace scope, all the way to the edge.

The edge was somewhere beyond the crest of the Vosges Mountains. Farman couldn't understand it. He'd sent those rockets straight as bullets into that formation, proximities primed and warheads armed. They should have climbed right up those Germans' tailpipes and fireballed and wiped those planes from the sky like tinder touched by flame. It hadn't happened.

He brought *Pika-Don* around. On the map scope he found again the position where the German planes had been. They didn't show on the airspace view—what could possibly be wrong with the radar—but they would still be close to where he'd seen them last, and he still had four rockets left. On the airspace scope, the tracks of rockets one and six ended in tiny sparks as their propellants exhausted and their automatic destructs melted them to vapor. He turned *Pika-Don*'s nose down. He armed the warheads, primed the proximities. This time he wouldn't miss.

He saw the German planes from ten miles away. He launched rockets two and five from a distance of five miles. Two seconds later, he launched three and four and turned away in a high-G immelmann. His G-suit seized him like a hand—squeezed, relaxed, and squeezed again as he threw *Pika-Don* into a long, circling curve. The airspace scope flickered, re-oriented itself. His four rockets traced bright streaks across its face.

Explode! he thought. *Explode!*

They didn't. They traced their paths out to the scope's edge. Their destruct mechanisms turned them to vapor. Ahead of him now, again, he could see the disorganized swarm of the jagdstaffel. He hadn't touched one of them. And they still didn't show on the airspace scope.

Farman swore with self-directed disgust. He should have thought of it. Those planes were invisible to radar. They didn't have enough metal among them to make a decent tin can, so his radar equipment rejected the signals they reflected as static. For the same reason, the proximities hadn't worked. The rockets could have passed right through the formation—probably had—without being triggered. As far as the proximities were concerned, they'd flown through empty air. He might as well have tried to shoot down a cloud.

He turned west, back to base. He located the field with the map scope. He had enough fuel to get there, and some to spare. A thought trickled through his mind about the dinosaurs—how their bodies had been perfectly adapted to the world they lived in, and when the world changed their bodies had not been able to adjust to the changes. So they died.

Pika-Don was like that—a flying *Tyrannosaurus rex* whose world now gave it only insects for food.

"Yeah. We saw the whole action," Blake said. He sat with his back against the hangar wall, a wine bottle close to his hand. The sun was bright and the fields were green. A light breeze stirred.

The escadrille had come back a half hour after Farman landed. Farman had hesitated, but then went out to face Deveraux. He was not eager for the confrontation.

Deveraux was philosophically gentle. "You have seen now, M'sieu, the rockets you carried were not an adequate armament for combat situations. Now, if you will show our mechanics where you think it would be best to mount the machine guns they . . ."

"*Pika-Don* flies faster than bullets," Farman said. He kicked at a ridge of dirt between wheel ruts. The dirt was hard, but it broke on the third try. "I even heard of a guy that got ahead of his own bullets and shot himself down. And his plane was a lot slower than mine." He shook his head—looked back toward where *Pika-Don* crouched low to the ground, sleek and sinister-looking, totally useless. "Might as well let her rot there."

He kicked the loosened clod off into the grass.

About eleven o'clock, Blake got a bottle of wine from Henri. It was plain peasant's wine, but that was all right. They sat in the narrow noontide shade of a hangar and worked on it.

"You've got to get in close before you shoot," Blake said. "I don't know where you learned combat, but it didn't look like you learned much. You flew at their formation so fast they wouldn't of seen you until you broke right through 'em, but you shot those rockets from a couple of miles away. You can't hit anything at that kind of range."

"I thought I could," Farman said. "And with the kind of warheads they had, it's a good idea to have a few miles distance when they go off."

"You don't think you're funning me with that, do you?" Blake said. He sat up straight—looked at Farman. "Nothing scatters shrapnel that wide."

Farman helped himself from the bottle. "My rockets would have done more than just scatter shrapnel, if they'd gone off."

"Not much good if you've got to shoot 'em from so far off you can't hit the target," Blake said.

It was no use trying again to explain target-seeking missiles. Anyway, they hadn't worked. He'd finally figured that out, too. Their heat-seeking elements had been designed to track on a hot jet's exhaust, or the meteor-flame of a ballistic warhead. All the German planes were putting out was the feeble warmth of a piston engine. That wasn't enough. If he was going to do any good in this war, it wasn't going to be with *Pika-Don*. "Harry, I want you to check me out on your plane."

"Huh?"

"My plane's useless. She hasn't any teeth left," Farman said. "If I'm going to do any more fighting, it's going to be in a plane like yours. I've got more flying hours than all of you put together, but I don't have any cockpit time in your—" He almost called them box kites. "I want you to show me how it flies."

Blake shrugged. "One plane's pretty much like another. They've all got their tricks—like these Nieuports, you don't want to do much diving in them; takes the fabric off the top wings every time. But aside from that the only way you get the feel is by flying 'em."

They walked out to Blake's Nieuport. It looked about as airworthy as a Model T Ford. Farman had a little trouble climbing up until Blake showed him the footholds. It was cramped in the cockpit, and the wicker seat was hard.

Blake stood on a packing crate and leaned over the coaming.

Farman put his hand on the stick. That was what it was—an erect rod sticking up between his knees. He'd never seen one like it before. He tried moving it, and it moved with the smoothness of a spoon in a gluepot. "Do you have to fight it like this all the time?" he asked.

"Takes some getting used to," Blake said. "It's easier when she's flying, though."

Farman turned his attention to the instruments. They were a haphazard assortment of circular dials, unevenly distributed, and except for one big dial straight in front of him there was no apparent priority of position given to the more important ones—whichever ones they were. They were all identified, the words lettered across their faces, but the words were French.

"That's the oil pressure," Blake said, tapping the glass in front of a dial. "And that's r.p.m., and that's fuel mixture."

"Oil pressure. Is that important?"

Blake looked at him strangely. "You say you've been flying . . . *how* long? And you don't know oil pressure?"

"I've never flown a piston engine craft," Farman said. "*Pika-Don* has a different kind. Is it important?"

"Your engine doesn't work too good without it."

"And—fuel mixture, did you say?" Farman asked, putting his finger to the dial Blake had indicated. He was careful not to ask if it was important, though he wasn't sure what difference it made. Mixed with what, he wondered to himself.

"Right," Blake said. "And this here's your compass—don't trust it too far—and that's the altimeter, and here's the gas gauge."

At least those were instruments Farman understood.

But he frowned at the altimeter. "Is that the highest this can fly?"

"Those are meters, not feet," Blake said. "This crate can go up as high as I can breathe. Sixteen . . . eighteen thousand feet." He pointed into the cockpit again. "This here's the switch, and that's the throttle, and that's the mixture control."

Farman touched them, one by one, trying to get their feel. His hand encountered a small plumb bob dangling from a cord. "Good-luck charm?" he asked.

Blake laughed. "Yeah, it's good luck all right. Without it I could be flying upside down and not know it."

"Don't you have a turn-and-bank indicator?" Farman wondered.

"Mister, that *is* my turn-and-bank indicator."

"Oh," Farman said, feeling foolish. But how could he have known?

"And these here," Blake went on, unnoticing, "that one tightens the flying wires, and that one the landing wires."

"What kind of wires?"

"Some wires you want tight when you're flying, and some others when you're coming in to land. If you don't, you stand a good chance of coming apart at the wrong time."

"Oh." Flying a Nieuport wasn't going to be as easy as he'd thought. It would be like trying to ride horseback after driving cars all your life. "My plane doesn't have wires."

"What holds it together?" Blake asked.

Farman ignored him. He was thinking about driving a car, and some of his confidence came back. This Nieuport was a lot different from *Pika-Don*, but her engine wasn't too much different from the one in the BMW he'd had in another place and time—more primitive, maybe, but it

worked on the same principles. He could handle a gasoline engine all right.

"Where's the starter?" he asked.

Blake frowned, as if he didn't understand. Then a wry
grin cracked his face. He nodded forward—pointed to the
propeller's blade. "Right there," he said.

Half a minute later Farman was looking forward
through the blur of a spinning propeller. He felt the blast
of air on his face, and the stench of exhaust made him
want to retch. The oil-pressure gauge worked up. He
experimented with throttle settings and fuel-mixture ad-
justments, trying to learn something about how it handled. It occurred to him that his BMW had two or three
times the horsepower this thing had.

Blake handed him a helmet and goggles. Farman put
them on. "Taxi her around a bit, until you get the feel,"
Blake yelled through the engine's blatting. Farman nodded, and Blake bent to pull the chocks from in front of the
wheels; one side and then—slipping quickly underneath
—the other. The Nieuport lurched forward even before
Farman advanced the throttle. It bumped clumsily over
the grass.

The thing had no brakes, so when he advanced the
throttle again she hurtled forward, bumping and thump-
ing across the field. The airspeed indicator began to show
readings. The bumping got worse. He edged the throttle
forward a little more. Except for the jouncing and that
awful smell, it wasn't much different from driving a car.

The tail came up. It startled him, and it was almost by
reflex—seeing the horizon lift in front of him—that
Farman pulled the stick back. The bumping stopped as if
it were shut off. The engine's sound changed, and airspeed began to slacken. The silly Model T was airborne.
He shoved the throttle forward and tried to level out. It
shouldn't have been flying at this speed—he'd driven his

BMW faster than this, and his BMW was a lot more streamlined.

He was beyond the field's edge now, with a rise of ground ahead of him. He tried to turn, but the Nieuport resisted. He pulled the stick back to clear the hill's crest. The airspeed meter started to unwind. He got over the hill with a few yards to spare, but airspeed was falling back toward zero. He tried to level out again; it wasn't easy to do without an artificial horizon on the instrument panel. The real horizon was rocking back and footh, up and down, and drifting sidewise. He tried turning the other way, and she turned easily but she also nosed down. He hauled back on the stick, swearing loudly. How any man could fly a crazy, contrary thing like this was more than he could understand.

The ground wheeled under him. The engine's sound changed, became a snarl, then a sputter. Wildly, he looked for a place to put down, but there was nothing but orchard under him as far as he could see—which wasn't far because the plane had nosed down again. A queasy, liquid feel began in his stomach, and the stench from the engine didn't help it any.

The engine chose that moment to quit. For a long time—it couldn't really have been more than a few seconds—the only sound was the whisper of air against the wings. Then the Nieuport stalled and plunged down among the trees. Branches snapped and the wings buckled. The Nieuport came to rest midway between the treetops and the ground. It dangled there, swaying a little in the gentle breeze. After a while, Farman thought to turn off the ignition, to reduce the danger of fire. After another while, he began to think about how to climb down.

He met Blake and half a dozen other men before he got out of the orchard. They went back to the Nieuport. Blake looked up at the wreck among the tree branches, made an angry noise that might have been extremely basic English, or it might not, and walked away.

Farman started to go after him but then thought better of it. Another tree branch cracked and the Nieuport sagged a few feet closer to the ground. Farman looked up at the mess one more time, then turned away and followed Blake. It was a long walk back to the field.

Blake was given another Nieuport. The escadrille had several replacements ready—craft that had been sent down from an escadrille in the Somme region that had switched to Spads. The older Nieuports were still good enough for this less active section of the front. Blake spent the rest of the day and all the next with the mechanics, checking it out.

Farman spent the time poking around *Pika-Don*, trying to figure a way she could still be used. There was a space where a Vickers gun could be fitted if he took out the infrared sensor unit, but working out a trigger linkage was beyond him; every cubic inch inside *Pika-Don* was occupied by one or another piece of vital equipment. And at Mach 2 an orifice the size of a .30-caliber muzzle might be enough to blow the plane apart.

The only other thing he could think of was that the radars were powerful enough to fry a man dead, but it didn't seem likely that Bruno Keyserling would hold still for the hour or two needed for the job.

He gave up. *Pika-Don* was useless. Reluctantly, he resigned himself to asking Deveraux for assignment to a flight school. It would mean swallowing a lot of pride, but if he was going to shoot Keyserling out of the sky, he'd have to learn how to fly a Nieuport.

When the escadrille came back from a patrol, he went out to talk with the Frenchman. Deveraux came toward him, helmet bunched in a still-gloved hand. "I am sorry, M'sieu," he said gravely. He laid his empty hand on Farman's shoulder. "Your friend . . . your countryman . . ."

The patrol had run into a flock of Albatrosses, Keyserling in the lead. No one had seen Blake go down, but several planes had been seen falling, burning like meteors. When the dogfight broke off and the flight had reformed, Blake wasn't with them.

Farman's mind became like cold iron as he heard Deveraux recite the plain, unchangeable facts. It shouldn't have struck him so hard, but Blake was a man he'd known, a man he'd talked with. All the other men here, even Deveraux, were strangers.

"Did anyone see a parachute?"

"M'sieu, such things do not work," Deveraux said. "We do not use them. They catch on the wires. For men in the balloons, perhaps such things can be used, but not for us. Our aeroplane is hit in its vitals, we go down."

"You shouldn't build them with so many wires, then."

Deveraux's reply was a Gallic shrug. "Perhaps not, M'sieu. But they are what hold our aeroplanes together."

"The German planes, too?" Farman asked in a suddenly different voice.

"Of course, M'sieu."

"Get me some kerosene," Farman said.

"Paraffin? Of course, M'sieu. And if you will show the mechanics where to fasten the machine guns they . . ."

Farman shook his head. "I don't need guns. Just get me the kerosene. I'll do the rest. And when I'm done with 'em on this front, I'll go up the line and clean out the rest of 'em."

"Of course, M'sieu," Deveraux said without irony.

Not that Farman cared. This time he'd do what he said he could do. He knew it. "Ten thousand gallons," he said.

Mid-August came, and *Pika-Don* was fueled again.
Reports and rumors had been coming down from other
sectors of the front that American troops were somewhere in the fighting.

Pika-Don lifted into a sky as clean as polished glass.
Later in the day there might be a scatter of cumulus tufts,
but it was not yet mid-morning. "It is not a good day for
fighting," Deveraux had said. "One can make use of the
clouds."

It would be a good day for observation planes, though,
so the German patrols would be out. And, Farman thought
savagely, there'd be fighting enough. He'd see to that.

Once he'd shifted to lateral flight, he didn't try for
altitude. *Pika-Don* would guzzle fuel faster at low levels,
but he didn't figure the mission to take long. The German
field was less than thirty miles away. He fixed its location
on the map scope and sent *Pika-Don* toward it at full
thrust. *Pika-Don* began to gain altitude, but at ten
thousand feet, with the Machmeter moving up past 1.75
he leveled her off and turned her downward along a
trajectory that would bring her to ground level just as he
reached the German field.

It was almost perfectly calculated. He saw the field
ahead of him. It was small—he'd seen pastures that were
bigger—and he started to pull out of his descent. He
passed over the field with just enough altitude to clear the
trees on the far side. It took less than a second—the
Machmeter said 2.5, and skin temperature was going up
fast. He took *Pika-Don* a few hundred feet up and brought
her around—lined her up on the field with the map
scope's help—and brought her down again for another
pass. This time she flew straight at the open mouth of a
hangar in the middle of a row of hangars on the far side of
the field.

He brought *Pika-Don* around one more time, but this time he stayed a thousand feet up and kept off to one side of the field. He looked down and felt the satisfaction of a kid who'd just stomped an anthill. Wreckage was still flying through the air. He didn't need rockets. He didn't need machine guns. All he had to have was *Pika-Don* herself.

He turned her south toward the Swiss border. He had seen only a few planes on the ground, which meant that most of them were out on patrol.

Heading south, he took *Pika-Don* up to eighteen thousand feet. On a day like this, with no clouds to hide in, the best altitude for a German patrol would be up close to the operational ceiling. Even if no altitude advantage could be gained, at least the advantage would not be lost to a higher-flying French patrol.

The map scope showed the Swiss border. Farman brought *Pika-Don* around. The front was not hard to find. It was a sinuous gash across the land, like a bloodless wound. He followed it north, staying to the German side. He watched the sky ahead of him.

He flew the course to the Vosges Mountains at Mach 1.5, partly to save fuel and to minimize the skin-temperature problem; flying this low, the air was a lot thicker than *Pika-Don* was built to fly in. His main reason, though, was that even at Mach 1.5 he was flying through a lot of airspace. With no more sophisticated target-finding equipment than his own bare eyes, he could pass within a mile or less of a German patrol and not see it. Flying as slowly as he could improved his chances.

The mountains rose ahead of him. They weren't very high mountains; their crests lay well below him. He caught sight of the German patrol as he turned *Pika-Don* for another run south.

They were a few hundred yards higher than he was, and so small with distance he'd have thought they were birds except that birds didn't fly this high, nor did birds fly in a neatly stacked Junck's row formation. They hung suspended in the sky, like fleck-marks on a window, and if it hadn't been for their formation he wouldn't have known their direction of flight. They were flying south, as he was now—patrolling the front, as he was.

And they were close—too close. If he turned toward them, they'd be inside the radius of his turn. He'd cross their path in front of them like a black cat, warning them. He mind-fixed their position on the map scope and turned away.

Come at them from eight o'clock, he decided. That would be the best angle. On the outward arc of his circle he took *Pika-Don* up to thirty thousand feet. Then, as *Pika-Don* started to come around for the approach, he started down, full thrust in all three engines. The Mach-meter climbed to 2.0, then 2.5. It edged toward 3.0, trembling. It would mean a heating problem in this soup-thick air, but it wouldn't be for long.

The patrol was almost exactly where he'd seen it before. There hadn't been time for it to move far. With only a small correction *Pika-Don* was driving down toward it like a lance, target-true. The insect-speck planes became recognizable shapes, then rapidly expanded. They ballooned to their full size in a flash and he was almost on top of them.

At the last instant, he moved the controls just enough to avoid collision—passed behind them so close he had a glimpse of round knobs bulging from the cockpits just behind the upper wings—pilots' helmeted heads—and yes! at the bottom of the stack, leading the flight, the purple Albatross of Bruno Keyserling.

Then the whole flight was somewhere behind him.

Farman reduced thrust and put *Pika-Don* into a steep climb, over on her back, and down again to level out into the airspace he'd flown through before.

It was all changed. The sky was full of junk, as if someone had emptied a barrel of trash. Fluttering wing sections, bashed fuselages, masses of twisted wreckage without any shape he could recognize. He saw a wingless fuselage falling a-tumble, like a crippled dragonfly. It was all purple, with bits of white on the shattered engine cowl. *Got him!*

And there wasn't a whole plane left in the sky. They hadn't been built to survive the impact of *Pika-Don*'s shock wave. Just like the hangars at their field which had exploded when he buzzed them.

He started to curve southward again. He'd tasted blood, wanted more. He'd hardly begun the turn when a whump shook *Pika-Don* and the sky wheeled crazily and the engine function instruments erupted with a Christmas tree of red lights as if engine two had gobbled something that didn't digest too well. (Part of an airplane? Part of a man?) Some of the lights flashed panic, others glared firmly at his eyes. The horizon outside was tipping up on edge, falling over, tipping up again. The controls felt numb in his hands.

Farman knew the drill. When a plane as hot as this one went bad, you got out if you could. At Mach 2 you could hit the ground in less than thirty seconds. He slapped the eject button—felt the rockets blast him upward. A moment later the instrument panel broke away and the seat's firm pressure on his back and thighs were gone. He was tumbling like a wobbling top in midair, suddenly no longer enclosed in several million dollars' worth of airplane. There was the teeth-cracking shock of his chute coming open, and abruptly the confusion of too many

things happening too fast stopped. He looked all around
for some trace of *Pika-Don*, but there wasn't any.

He tugged at the shrouds to spill air from the chute and
drift him westward toward the French lines. The wind
was doing some of it, but not enough. A line of planes
came toward him. He held his breath, thinking of a school
of sharks nosing in toward a man cast overboard. But
then he saw the French markings on their wings and
sides. They were Nieuports, and the pilot of the leading
plane waved. Farman waved back. The flight came on. It
circled him once and then curved off. They stayed in sight,
though, following him down. When flak bursts started to
puff around him, they went down to strafe the German
trenches.

He spilled another dollop of air from his chute. He was
over the French lines now. He could see the men in the
trenches looking up at him. He floated down toward
them, closer and closer. Then, very abruptly, he was
down—down among the trenches and barbed wire of the
French Seventh Army. He sprawled in the greasy mud of
a shell hole. The chute started to drag him, but it caught
on a tangle of wire and collapsed.

He got to his hands and knees, fumbling with the
parachute harness. A bullet snapped past his ear. He
flattened. The Nieuports dived on the German trenches
again.

He struggled out of the harness and started to crawl in
the direction of the nearest trench. It wasn't far. He
scraped the dirt with his belt buckle all the way. Bullets
whipped past him like deadly mosquitoes. The soldiers in
the trenches reached out to pull him down.

They hugged him. They mobbed around him. There
must have been thousands of men in that trench to
celebrate the man who'd brought down Bruno Keyserling.
Someone pressed a cup of wine into his hands—a soldier

in dirty clothes, with mud on his brow and a matted beard. Farman drank gratefully.

After a while, he sat down and just sat there, dead inside. He looked at the dirt wall a few inches from his eyes. The empty cup dangled from his hand. *Pika-Don* was gone, and nothing he could do would rebuild her. Suddenly he was just an ordinary man. He couldn't even fly any more. *Pika-Don* had been the only plane in this age that he knew how to fly, and *Pika-Don* was gone.

He wasn't aware of the passage of time, but only of the heat and dust and the smell of a trench that had been lived in too long by unwashed men. He didn't know what he was going to do. But after a time, the wine began to have its effect. A trickle of life came back into him.

Slowly, he got to his feet. The start of a smile quirked his mouth. On second thought, no, he wasn't just an ordinary man.

The war would be over in a few months. Maybe he didn't know what he'd do, but . . .

The soldier who'd given him the wine was standing a few feet away. Farman held himself crisply erect. It occurred to him the man probably didn't know a word of English.

"How do I get back to America?" he asked, and grinned at the soldier's incomprehension.

A man from the future ought to have *some* advantage over the natives!

THE PERMANENT
IMPLOSION

The fire was out. It had taken two shots, but now it was out and the well was capped. Workmen were beginning to cut up the shoved-aside wreck of the heat-buckled drill rig. A bulldozer bumbled ponderously around, scraping up random debris.

Mick Candido sat on the truck's running board and worked on his pipe. It was always going out, or the tobacco was getting too tightly packed in the bowl to burn right, or something. His body was sticky with sweat under his clothes. He was tired. It had been a rough day.

Money in the bank, though.

A thump and then a scuffing rustle back in the truck's body told him Ken Storch had heaved another roll of hose aboard. One more to go, he thought—and then the pump. Then they'd be loaded, ready to go. The other trucks had already gone.

He gave up on his pipe. He leaned back and watched the helicopter that had appeared above the wind-scalloped, treeless hills. It was down low to the horizon, no larger than a gnat, and coming this way. The sky was clean—the rich blue of the high plains, and a few white featherwisps of cirrus. He pulled out his tobacco pouch, zipped his pipe inside, and returned it to his pocket.

Another thump hit the truck bed. Ken Storch came

around the side. His shirt was dark with sweat. He brushed hair back from his forehead with a grimy hand. "All done but the pump, Mr. Candido."

Candido stood up. He was a big man—not so much in height as in muscular mass; broad shoulders, thick body, and powerful legs and arms. He'd been first-string center on the football team at East Texas College for three years, and he hadn't done bad on the wrestling squad, either.

"Right," he said, and they walked down the hill to the mud-plastered trench. A few hours ago it had been full of water like a swimming pool; now a few puddles glistened slickly in the deeper hollows. They'd had to use almost all of it.

Together, they lifted the pump and carried it back up the slope. It weighed one hundred and sixty pounds; not much for a pump, but it could throw four hoses of water at once—hard. You could depend on it to keep on throwing water, too, which was a necessary thing when you were in your klansman's suit—asbestos hood and coverall—trying to get the dynamite in close enough to the torch so the blast would snuff it. Times like those, Niagara itself couldn't be too much water; it steamed off your back like smoke.

They raised the pump over the tailgate and slid it into the truck until it pushed up against the wet rolls of hose. Hardly out of breath at all, Candido folded the tailgate up and hooked it shut, then rattled it to make sure it was fast.

"Back to the motel?" Storch asked.

"Not yet," Candido said. He was watching the helicopter again. It was a lot closer now. He could see the blurry sweep of its rotors, and he was thinking of the long, bumpy ride back to Sand Springs—three and a half hours on dirt tracks you could call roads only in the sense that jeeps and trucks with lug tires could struggle over them.

If the copter was going to land here—and it looked that way—and if it was going back almost right away, maybe he could cadge a ride aboard. If they had space for another passenger.

He thought about his room in the motel. It was air-conditioned. He needed a shower and fresh clothes. He needed another treatment of salve on the burns he'd got in spite of his klansman's suit. And maybe a big steak dinner, and then a good long sleep.

He always felt that way when a job was done.

The helicopter settled on its wheels with a blast of wind. Dust and sand flew. Before the rotors had stopped turning, the door opened and a man stepped down. He wore a business suit, but the helicopter was an Army machine: painted ugly green, with a white serial number stenciled on its flank like the brand on a cow.

The man came toward the truck. He walked carefully, watching the ground where he set his feet. He wore ordinary street shoes with low sides. The sand gave way under his feet.

"Hello," he said. "I'm looking for Michael Candido. You work for him?" He nodded to the truck. *Wellfire Blasting, Inc.* it said in flame-limned letters on the door. *Fort Worth, Texas.*

"I *am* him," Mick Candido said.

"Good," the man said. "We need you. I just came from Denver."

He said it as if Denver meant something.

"I'm from Fort Worth, myself," Candido said. "What did you say your name was?"

"Hugh Trask," the man said hurriedly, as if the business of names was a nuisance to be got out of the way as fast as possible. "Civil Defense, Denver District." He was somewhere in his forties. His jowls had a meaty, thick look.

"Pleased to meet," Candido said. He stuck out his hand. It was filthy. "Now, business?"

"You mean you haven't heard? You don't know about the whirlwind?"

"Friend," Candido said, "when I'm out on a job, I don't hear nothing but job and I don't think anything but job."

"Well, we need a man with your experience," Trask said. He nodded back toward the helicopter. "Will you take the job?"

Candido frowned. "Since when did they have a field near Denver?"

"Field?" Trask's face was blank.

"Oil field," Candido said. "Wells."

"Oh!" Trask understood now. "But it's not an oil field. It's not even a fire. What we want you for . . . well, it's complicated." He waved a hand to the helicopter. "I'll tell you about it on the way."

Candido got out his pipe. He made sure he could draw through it, then packed tobacco in the bowl. He took his time. "I'll accept a ride back to town," he said, making it sound like a major concession. "You've got me curious, all right. I'll listen." He turned to Ken Storch. "You take the truck in," he said.

"Then you'll take the job?" Hugh Trask asked anxiously.

"I said I'll listen," Candido said. He got his pipe lighted and broke the match and dropped the pieces in the pocket of his denim shirt. "If I like how it sounds, we'll talk business." He started upslope toward the helicopter. Trask tagged alongside. "You're authorized to sign a contract?" he asked Trask.

Trask was out of breath, though the climb wasn't steep. Behind them, Storch got the truck started. There was a grind of gears.

"I don't know," Trask said. "I think so. We have a

disaster fund, and this . . . well, this is that, for sure. But surely business arrangements can wait. This . . . this is important."

The door in the helicopter's side was open. Candido grabbed the hand-hold inside, stuck his foot in the toe-step, climbed inside. Out of the bright sunlight, it was like suddenly going blind. He groped and found a seat and sat down. "It's always a good time to talk business," he said. The seat was much too small for him, but he was accustomed to that. Most seats were. "Business happens to be my game."

"Lift up, Mr. Trask?" someone asked from up forward.

"Yes. Take off," Trask said. He was buckling into the seat across the narrow aisle. Candido found his own seat belt. Its straps were just barely long enough to reach around him. The helicopter's idling engine roared up to power. A shutterlike shadow flicked across the forward window, then came again—then again and again. The helicopter vibrated, buzzed, surged, and the ground dropped away. After a moment, Candido could look out the window beside him and see, far below, the tiny fittings of the wellhead and the wrecked drill rig and the blackened earth in a circle around it like a blot of ink, and the men and the bulldozer swarming over the scene, like wonderfully perfect toys.

The low, rippling hills ridged the land like a lethargic, heaving sea. Candido watched them drift past underneath and listened to the engine's noise and heard Trask tell of the thing that had happened near Denver.

No one would ever know exactly what happened. The only men who might have known had vanished—devoured by the thing they'd created. There'd been a research laboratory on the plain northeast of Boulder; Civil Defense hadn't yet found out what it had been doing.

Anyway, it was gone now, and where it had been, the center of a vast, powerful whirlwind wheeled and roared. Everything for miles around had been swept up by it—smashed, shredded, uprooted, and carried away.

"This is the significant point," Trask said. "Something in the center of that whirlwind . . . something is drawing air toward it, very forcefully. That's what's causing the whirlwind."

"Hm-m-m," Candido said. "Where's all this air going?"

"Huh?" Trask's brows squeezed together like rope twisted tight, beginning to bunch. "Why, I hadn't thought about that. However, I suppose our physicists know, and it makes no difference. The thing we want you for— you're experienced in the handling of explosives under . . . well, unusual conditions. Our physicists believe that the shock of an explosion close to the center of the whirlwind will destroy the . . . uh, the condition that is causing it."

Candido thought a minute. "How fast did you say the wind's going?"

Below them, the land opened into a deep, gully-carved valley. The kinked and twisting channel was white-crusted—dry as a skillet. Eye-glazing light shimmered on arid promontories. Then the land lifted again and the valley fell behind. Over the rolling plain, dust devils twisted.

"Understand," Trask said, "we haven't been able to get close to the center to measure the wind velocities there. And there's too much dust for us to estimate by observing things caught in it. But about five hundred yards out, it seems to be blowing steadily at a hundred and forty miles an hour."

Candido grunted as if he'd taken a fist in the gut. "Not what I call a breeze," he said. "Take something big to put a dent in it. What about these physicists of yours? How much of a blast do they figure it needs?"

"I don't handle technical details," Trask said. "I'm an administrator. I have no idea. I haven't discussed it with them."

"Maybe it'll make a difference whether I take the job or don't," Candido said. "Usually my price goes up five thousand for every hundredweight of Hercules over three hundred pounds. If it's over a ton, I don't even talk to you. I wave good-by. That's how it's sounding right now."

Far ahead now, they could see the town, Sand Springs. It was a patch of green on the scrub-dotted land, nestled among the naked hills, tiny with distance—too small, it seemed, for a town; but over it stood the toy-size water tower on spread legs. Ten, fifteen miles.

"They tell me it might not take a particularly large blast," Trask said. "They believe the thing that's causing it involves a delicate balance of forces, and only a small additional force would upset it."

"They think that, huh?" Candido said. He thought for a while, as the town came gradually nearer and nearer, hillcrest after hillcrest. He'd just finished a job, and it was money in the bank, and no new jobs were shaping up. This whirlwind wasn't his usual line of work, exactly, but it did have ginger in it—something different. Something new, a challenge, like the time he was a boy and a kid three years older had scratched a line in the dirt and said for him to cross it. He'd looked the kid up and down, taken his measure, and stepped across the line and smashed him flat. He began thinking about how to get to the center of that roaring wind.

"Naturally, you'll be given all the assistance we can," Trask said. He was talking quickly, anxious, trying to persuade him. "And all the equipment you need. This . . . this is a disaster. It's got to be stopped. Soon."

"Well," Candido said, and paused to read Trask's face. The man was frantic—maybe a little desperate, even— but that didn't help much when you were haggling with the government. Uncle Sam was a tough old skinflint when it came to bargaining, and even if you got it down in black and white on good crisp parchment, you still couldn't be sure the deal would stick. Just the same . . .

"I don't say I'll take the job," Candido said, "but I'll admit to being interested. Anyway, I'll go as far as Denver and look it over. Good enough?"

Trask called forward for the helicopter to change course and fly to Denver. Candido countermanded the instruction and obliged them to land at the edge of the town. It was a short walk to the motel. There he showered, shaved, and got a change of clothes. He packed, left word for his crew to bring the trucks down to Denver, caught a sandwich and coffee at the nearest cafe, and walked back to the helicopter.

The pilot already had the engine going when he climbed aboard. As soon as he was safety-belted in a seat the rotors began to turn and they were airborne. It was late afternoon. It was night before they arrived over Denver.

The helicopter had curved far east over the plains and approached the city on westward course. The wind gusted roughly, jolting the craft. Thick clouds clotted the sky. The city's light filled the overcast with a glow like embering fire.

Trask had telephoned of their coming before they left Sand Springs, and in spite of the lateness of the hour there were men waiting in a conference room in the Centennial Hotel. The streets were wet with rain.

Candido glanced at the blank blackboard and the board next to it on which a topographic quadrangle map had been tacked. One of the men had a piece of chalk in his hand. He was almost bald and he wore rimless glasses and he was thin. His shirt was open at the throat. His tweed had leather patches at the elbows. A waiter arrived with a large pot of coffee and a half dozen cups. Candido remembered how long it had been since he'd been near a bed. He got out his pipe, stuffed the bowl, dabbed a match over it until the tobacco caught.

The man with the piece of chalk was Willard L'Heuroux, and he was a physicist from the University at Boulder. He rubbed the end of the chalk with his thumb. The palp of his thumb was white with the dust. He had only a few details to add to the information Trask had given already, but Candido listened carefully. Details could be important—even small ones.

The center of the whirlwind was over a rise of ground named Gunbarrel Hill. It showed clearly on the quadrangle map, even to someone who didn't know how to read contour lines. Candido knew how. He studied the few roads that gridded the area and thought about the wind that was strong even here, twenty or thirty miles away. He didn't like it.

L'Heuroux had some high-altitude photographs of the whirlwind. It was a vast, round, doughnut-like cloud, like a hurricane but with almost no eye. Storm clouds surrounded the toroid, and the photoplane's pilot had reported a powerful downdraft even at sixty thousand feet. Air was flowing toward the whirlwind's center from all directions—from above as well as from all points of the compass.

That was all the fact they had. The rest was theory, as unprovable as the noise an unseen tree makes in falling. But one of the research problems being worked on in the lab, the one the whirlwind had smashed, had been a direct investigation of an aspect of Mach's principle—that in a universe with no material objects all points are identical, since there can be no reference points on which to base a system of coordinates. No one really questioned this concept any more—at least, no one of the proper sophistication.

"Pardon me," Candido said. "I always thought we've got a universe with a few material objects lying around."

"Quite true," L'Heuroux said. "However, if we should choose to ignore that point—and mathematically I assure you it's very easy to do . . ."

Candido growled skeptically and rubbed his brows with the heels of his thumbs. "All right. Go on."

Well now, if all locations in the universe were identical, it naturally followed that transfer of objects from one place to another should be ridiculously simple, since obviously they were in both positions—among others— all the time. Of course, the real universe didn't precisely conform to the idealized scheme being utilized; some compensation had to be made. This had been one of the problems the laboratory was investigating. A secondary, more difficult problem had been to control selection of the non-different points which were being made congruent.

Maybe it was because he hadn't had a good night's sleep the last few days, but Candido couldn't grasp the concept. Like trying to gnaw fog, he thought. He added just enough cream to his coffee to lighten its blackness. He drank half the cup in one draught.

Maybe the coffee helped. At least he got the idea of the next part—that at the center of the whirlwind was a locus, a volume of space, which was simultaneously in two places. One was a few yards above the surface of Gunbarrel Hill. The other was . . . well, somewhere else. And since something more than ninety-nine per cent of the universe is interstellar space, what could be more logical but that the somewhere else should be such a region? And it was vacuum there—a vacuum more empty than any that could be made in any laboratory in the world. Nothing could be done to prevent the air contained within the congruent volume from escaping into the emptiness around it.

Candido's pipe had gone out some time ago. He opened his jackknife and pried the mess out of the bowl and dumped it in an ashtray. He started over.

"You figure a hard blast of Hercules will knock this thing off?"

"That is our belief," L'Heuroux said. "The whirlwind has destroyed all the equipment that created it. Therefore, the condition of congruency must be one that is self-maintaining. This would mean, we think, a moderately delicate balance of forces which an abrupt shock—such as a disturbance in the patterns of movement of the air molecules entering the sphere—would disrupt. At least, that is our hope."

"And I'm the guy to set the charge," Candido said. It was like someone had pulled the plug, he thought, and air was draining out of the world like water from a bathtub. If it was in the southern hemisphere, he thought, the whirlwind would be wheeling in the other direction—clockwise instead of counterclockwise. He wondered how long before there wasn't any air left. He began to know how goldfish feel when their bowl is smashed.

"All right," he said. "You've got your man. You supply the equipment—I'm set up for fires, not wind—not a wind like this, anyway—and I'll do the job. Two hundred thousand."

Trask's face was like a papier-mâché mask, his eyes staring through the holes. "That's rather high," he said. His voice was a little unsteady.

"It's dangerous work," Candido said.

"But our budget isn't a tenth of that."

"Call Uncle," Candido said. "Two hundred thousand. I

figure that's pretty cheap for all the air you can breathe."

The corners of Trask's mouth twitched as if he felt pain. He stood up. "If you'll excuse me," he said, and left the room.

Candido waited. Nobody spoke. Trask was gone ten minutes. He came back and stood in the doorway. "I'm instructed to offer fifty thousand," he said. "It will mean asking Congress for a special appropriation, but we can offer that much."

"As a taxpayer, I think that's a good offer," Candido said. "As a businessman, I say it's no good. Two hundred thousand."

Trask met his eyes for a moment, then turned and went out again.

Candido turned his attention to L'Heuroux. "How long's it been blowing?"

"Three days," L'Heuroux said. "Two and a half. It began in the afternoon, day before yesterday."

"How long before we don't have any air left?" Candido asked.

To judge by the look on the physicist's face, it was something he hadn't thought of. "Why, I really don't know," L'Heuroux said. "I'd have to compute. I don't think we have the data. I assume what you mean is, how long before the air pressure drops below the level at which it can support life."

"That's close enough," Candido said.

"Otherwise," L'Heuroux said, as if Candido hadn't spoken, "I would have to say we'll never have lost all our atmosphere. As the air pressure drops, there would be less pressure forcing air into the congruency. Therefore, since the pressure drop would be progressive, an infinite length of time would have to pass before all our atmosphere was gone."

"If I can't breathe, I don't call it air," Candido said. "How long do you figure?"

Trask came back then. He sat down. "All right," he said. "Two hundred thousand."

"In writing," Candido said.

"All right. In writing. Tomorrow morning."

"Good enough," Candido said, satisfied. "That'll just about pay my income tax."

The wind blew gale force at the edge of Boulder. Houses had slashed roofs and trees lay uprooted. The tank's Diesel was a growl above the whirlwind's blast.

They'd spent a day getting ready—moving the tank down from the Army camp near Cheyenne and learning how to drive it and waiting for his crew to make it down from the Gas Hills. They'd come in last night. The tank weighed sixty-four tons and it had a low silhouette. Massive enough, Candido figured, that the wind wouldn't bother it too much. Ken Storch rode in the gunner's seat beside him, and L'Heuroux rode in the turret. Candido hoped the hatch lock would hold. He'd checked it and he thought it would, but if it didn't the wind would suck them out like marrow from a bone. He was mildly curious about what was on the other side of that congruency, but not so curious he wanted to go there.

Scraps of debris—some of them not small—skipped along the ground, sailed up into the air. A tree branch went by. A section of billboard touting Coors beer. Another advantage to the tank, it could move across country. It didn't have to keep to the grid pattern of roads. It could keep the wind at its back, if that was the only way it could move.

But here, still close to Boulder, he stayed on the road. It was easier going, and the wind wasn't strong enough to bother him yet, and it was tricky to drive with just the narrow slit of the periscope to see through. You could lose your bearings fast. He gripped the brake levers, now and then tugging a little at one or the other, keeping the machine on an even course down the middle of the road. They met no traffic. There was only the tank and the empty road. Rain squalls lashed the pavement and passed on. The wind screeched like a mountain lion in rage. Gusts made his ears pop, and he had to swallow to get his hearing right again.

The road turned, then turned again, and then they were grinding up the slope. Wind blasted on the tank's flank like a padded hammer, and the noise of it almost blotted out the sound of the laboring Diesel.

"What's the air pressure?" Candido asked.

"Twenty and six-tenths," L'Heuroux said, behind him.

He felt vibration in his bucket seat. He had to use the brakes a lot to keep the tank from drifting sidewise into the ditch. The tank's treads clawed the pavement. Scrabbled. Down to twenty and a half already, and still more than a mile to go. He could imagine the torn asphalt they were leaving behind them, even though he couldn't turn his periscope enough to see.

Then they were nearing the hillcrest, and here was the turn off to where the research lab had been. Candido hauled on the left brake lever and the left tread locked and the tank spun to the left and the wind hit the tank's side as if a shell had burst on the armor. Candido let up on the brake and the tank stopped turning; he upped the throttle and the Diesel's snarl raised its pitch a few notes and they ground forward into the drive.

The land was ripped bare like bones cleaned by carrion birds. Not even grass grew in the earth. Here and there, a wooden fencepost had held against the blast. That was all. Ahead, a little to the left of the road, the air was in violent turmoil. Debris and dust and cloud streamed inward from all directions. Candido stopped the tank and studied the epicenter, but he was too far away to make out anything clearly. He slacked the brakes and put in the clutch, and the tank lurched forward. "What's the pressure like?" he asked over his shoulder.

"Fifteen and seven-tenths," L'Heuroux said. The tank shuddered with the impact of wind. Candido kept his eyes on the center of the converging winds, only now and then glancing at the road. This road didn't have ditches at the verge; he didn't have to worry about getting caught in one of them. He did some mental calculations.

"It should be up around twenty-five," he said.

"Within a point or two of that," L'Heuroux said. "That's normal for this altitude."

Candido stopped the tank. "We don't go any closer," he said. The tank trembled in the wind's fury. The wind was an unending scream.

"Is something wrong?" L'Heuroux asked.

Candido could just barely see what was left of the laboratory building's foundation. He'd have liked to get closer, to study out the kind of ground he'd have to work over when they went in to plant the Hercules. Not now, though. Not with the pressure down there. His shoulders felt like they were wearing plaster casts. He felt a peculiar singing in his blood.

"Nothing's gone wrong yet," he said. "It would if we kept on going." He got the tank turned around. He gave the Diesel full throttle. It was like trying to probe bottom in quicksand. The tank didn't move. The Diesel didn't have any power. The wind drove against the tank, striking from just off the starboard bow. Its force was stronger than the Diesel.

"We don't go any closer without breathing equipment,"

Candido said. "And a supercharger on the engine. We're not getting enough air to breathe right, and if I'm any guess it's even thinner the closer you get to . . ." He let a gesture complete the sentence. "If we get much closer, we'd keel over. And we'd have our engine stall."

He got the tank turned to the left, fed power to the Diesel. They lumbered off the road. The ground was uneven. The tank bumped and jolted. The engine still didn't have much power, but they were going crosswind now instead of fighting it. He had to crab into it some, but that was possible. They made headway.

"Why, I hadn't considered that," L'Heuroux said.

"Didn't think you had," Candido said. "You're not in business. Did you get a figure for wind velocity?"

"Not a very dependable one. I think the equipment must be damaged."

"What's the figure you got?" Candido asked.

"Two hundred and ninety miles per hour," L'Heuroux said.

Candido twitched the right-hand brake lever, quartering them into the wind a little more steeply. He could feel the treads slip and jerk as they clawed for footing. Ahead, the land sloped gently downward. The wind sang its fury. Candido thought of all the air vanishing into that bottomless vacuum—air no man would ever breathe again.

The breathing equipment was no problem. Face masks and air tanks and a compressor were part of Candido's stock of equipment. A supercharger for the Diesel was not so easy.

Diesels weren't built for high-altitude work. Superchargers didn't exist. Candido catnapped most of the afternoon in his Boulder motel room while Trask and his subordinates telephoned everywhere, trying to locate something that would fill the need. They had trouble, Trask said, because a lot of wires were blown down.

Finally—it was almost five—they found one in Dayton. It was designed for a gasoline engine, but it could operate—not efficiently, but it could operate—at the tank Diesel's r.p.m. It was loaded on a jet transport at Wright-Patterson and flown west. Candido spent most of the night watching it being installed. They had to cut away some of the armor to make room for it, and then they had to build a housing for it to protect it from the wind and windborne objects. It screamed like a devil with its tail being stepped on. It was a jerry-rigged, makeshift assembly. Candido made sure he could control it. Finally, he was satisfied.

"All right," he said. "Now, will it do the job where we're going?"

The engineer managing the job was a hairy, scrawny man named Henry Janiszewski. "It's working as good as it ever will," he said, wiping his hands on a rag. "If you want more than that, you'll have to ask someone else." He rolled down his sleeves, exposing sergeant's stripes.

It was mid-morning now, and nobody had got much sleep. Trask merely looked dumb when asked. L'Heuroux, when they woke him and got him to understand through his drowsiness what the question was, didn't know either.

"We don't go near the whirlwind till we've tested it," Candido said.

"Tested it?" Trask asked. "How?"

"I want to know that engine works and gives power where the barometer says ten inches," Candido said. "If it's going to quit, I want it to quit while we're testing it—not while I'm in it, looking that wind in the eye."

"But where in heaven is there a pressure chamber large enough to take that"—L'Heuroux's hand flapped wildly in the direction of the tank—"that monster."

"Not heaven," Candido said. "Here. How should I know? Don't you?"

So another search began. It didn't take as long, this time. Not many big low-pressure chambers existed. Someone in Washington dug out a list of them, and there was one capacious enough in a missile factory in the foothills southwest of Denver, less than fifty miles away.

Candido made the ride down in the cab of the tank's carrier rig. He held his breathing equipment on his lap. Rain fell most of the way—slashing, hurricane rain. They were expected; the guard waved them through the gate and pointed them the way to go.

Big as it was, the pressure chamber was just barely big enough. The tank fitted inside like a chick in its egg. The pressure chamber and its massive vacuum pumps were part of the missile company's research equipment, and the whole rig-up had cost—Candido didn't catch how many hundred thousands. They were proud of how much it had cost. Candido cracked a grin and said it was a lot of cash to spend for nothing. They didn't get the joke. They explained earnestly that a really solid vacuum was a hard thing to get and to get a good one was worth a lot of money. Candido shrugged and they got to business.

He breathed canned air through his mask and kept the Diesel running while they pumped the chamber down to ten inches. They did it slowly, leaking some air back in to replenish the oxygen the Diesel burned. As the air got thinner, the Diesel's growl changed note. At just under fourteen inches, it began running rough. Candido cut in the supercharger. It smoothed out and stayed smooth the rest of the way down to ten.

He tried throttle settings all the way up the scale. It was hard to tell much—the Diesel kept running all right, but its sound meant nothing in the thin air. He cut the throttle back to idle, made sure the brakes were locked tight, and watched the few inches between the tank's foremost projection and the walls of the chamber, while gingerly, fractions at a time, he let in the clutch. The engine stalled.

It took several tries to get the Diesel started again, but finally it turned over. He advanced the throttle a little and tried the clutch again. The brakes still held. He kept on trying. He'd gone most of the way up the throttle settings before the tank even trembled when he let in the clutch. The throttle was almost against the stops when, finally, the tank strained feebly against the brakes—lurched an inch or two forward before Candido hastily opened the clutch.

It wasn't much of a test, but it would have to do. At least he could count on the Diesel to deliver power. Not much, but some. It was slushy, but not so bad he couldn't manage it. He opened the hatch, poked his head out, and signed to the man watching through the window. His ears felt the pressure change as they cracked the valves. Air leaked back into the chamber. A shrill whistle bit his ears. The tank was good enough, now, to risk taking it up to the whirlwind's center. It would still be a risk, but there were always risks. You took a chance every time you crossed the street.

They drove north again through rain and the new-fallen night. He slept in his motel room, woke early, and made sure all was ready for the day's work.

The explosive—a half-ton of high-nitro dynamite—was packed solidly in a lead container. The canister's top was thin, but its sides and bottom were heavy. The charge would be set down directly under the congruency. The blast would be upward, directly into it. Under the lid, a radio detonator nested among its wires like a spider in its web. L'Heuroux had taken photographs, and enlargements showed the center of the whirlwind as a large globe suspended ten feet off the ground, in which the turbulent wind swirled in a pattern different from that of the inward driving winds surrounding it. L'Heuroux had been disappointed that the various color sensitivities of the films and light filters he'd used had shown nothing to suggest the nature of the sphere. Candido couldn't have cared less. He made sure the rigging would hold the canister tightly in spite of the wind's force. He checked the mechanism that would set it on the ground. It would work all right.

Something clanged on the turret as he made the turn into the drive for the approach to the whirlwind's vortex. A tree branch, or something else, caught in the wind. He stopped the tank and locked the brakes. He unwrapped another stick of gum and added it to the wad already in his mouth. He slipped on his breather mask—made sure it fitted tight. Glancing over his shoulder, he saw Ken Storch already wearing his mask. L'Heuroux was fumbling with his.

He waited. Finally, the physicist signed he was ready. Candido turned forward again, slipped the brakes, and boosted the supercharger. The Diesel snarled. With a lurch, the tank advanced. A sudden, brief slash of rain rattled like bullets on the tank's side. Trickles of water dribbled in around the hatchways and around the turret. Cold wet dripped on Candido's neck. He had to yank the left brake handle constantly to hold the tank on the road. The tank boomed in the blast of the wind.

It got worse the nearer they came. The pinwheeling wind swept more steeply across the road and its force was magnified. The tank skidded and scuttled on the wind-polished earth; there'd been gravel on the road once, but no more. The parking lot, when they came to it, could be recognized only because it was flat and open while the land around it flowed unevenly. Candido gave it hardly a glance.

Not much was left of the lab's foundations—some

masses of concrete still bearing battered remnants of equipment they had been poured to support, a few fragments of cinder block embedded at the edges of a level concrete floor that lifted perhaps half a foot above ground level, a few steel reinforcing bars jutting out of the floor—twisted, bent, and snapped off: ugly stubs. Something carried in the wind caught momentarily against one of the longer bars. The bar wrenched, gave way, and the object broke and its fragments whipped away so swiftly the eye couldn't follow.

The sphere was ten or eleven feet above the floor, suspended, motionless. The wind drove into it, swirling everything trapped inside it into violent frenzy. Surfaces, tendrils, wisps, and solid things whirled and gyrated crazily, and Candido thought of the part-transparent, part-opaque marbles he had played with as a boy. The globe was like one of those marbles, wildly spinning, endlessly shifting form inside—or like a picture he'd seen of the planet Jupiter, the planet's globe banded like a zebra and the whole monstrous thing whirling all the way around every nine and a fraction hours. It dizzied the eye.

On the floor, a low, vaguely conical heap of rubbish had collected. Candido stopped the tank—made sure the brakes would hold against the wind. He studied the expanse of floor almost inch by inch, deciding how best to make the approach. It wasn't going to be easy. Those twisted steel rods and concrete piers could do nasty things to the tank's treads. He had to cross at least fifty feet of that mess.

After a while, he moved the tank to a new point of vantage. The floor looked just as bad from this angle. The wind would make trouble, too. It was like a maze game played with steel balls in a strong magnetic field, no mistakes allowed. He took the tank around to the other side of the foundation, pausing for a good look every few yards. There was no good way to get in—just some that weren't as bad as others. The wind forced jets in under the hatches. It was like being stabbed with icicles. The shrill whistlings were like red-hot needles in his ears.

He chose the best way he could find. He hoped the treads would hold up. It was all he could do. Slowly, as if feeling his way, he got the tank up on the platform. Moving only a few feet at a time, he advanced the machine across the concrete floor, twisting, backing and filling, crabbing carefully into the wind, and the wind was like something solid. The wind tried to shoulder the tank—sidewise, cornerwise, or anywise except the way he wanted to go—toward the globe, and the globe hovered closer, ever closer as he picked his way toward it. *Get thee behind me, Satan, and push!* he thought savagely. That was what the wind was doing. He fought it.

The rubbish under the sphere crunched and crushed under the treads like pith balls. Here, miraculously, the wind did not blow. Candido's ears popped. His head rang and he had no strength and his blood pounded strongly. He turned up the supercharger all the way, but still the Diesel's response to the throttle was soft. He knew what the trouble was, all right. He glanced back at L'Heuroux; the physicist held up seven fingers.

He turned back to the periscope, shrugging. Nothing he could do to change it. He maneuvered the tank forward and back until the debris had been flattened. He brought the tank inward once more, maneuvering until the tank's prow was as near to being directly under the sphere's center as his eye could gauge. He opened the clutch—let the engine idle; no need to lock the brakes here. He nodded to Storch.

The younger man had the controls of the explosives-handling rig. It was a makeshift: no manufacturer made a rig strong enough to hold against the wind, nor one that could be worked through the constricted ports intended for machine-gun muzzles. It had been a job to build. They'd had to make it flawless, perfect in operation. There'd be no getting out to make repairs while the wind raged, nor here in this semivacuum. It was all a man could do to hold to consciousness against the beating and the vagueness in his skull.

Storch handled the rig like he'd got a doctorate in rig-handling from MIT. Well, he should, Candido thought. He'd trained the man himself. Through the periscope, he watched the heavy beams extend, proffering the massive canister forward, then down until the canister's butt touched ground. The beams continued to droop lower and lower, until the long bolts slipped free of the flanges on the canister's sides. Now the beams drew back, slowly, like arthritic arms that had made an offering to a tyrannical god.

"All right," Storch said. His voice was muffled by his breathing mask.

Candido backed the tank away. He gave Storch time to get the rig retracted. He turned the tank—began to trace the way back through the maze. He couldn't go exactly the same way—some of the way he'd come was, going back, directly into the teeth of the wind. It was like trying to push through a mountain. Even if the Diesel had had full power—it didn't, not here, the air pressure so low—in spite of the supercharger it lacked the power to drive against that slamming wind. He found another way.

A hundred yards off, he turned the tank back to face the sphere. He looked at Storch—nodded. Storch unlocked the radio-detonator box. Candido didn't like using radio to set off a blast—you couldn't trust radio the way you could wires—but with the wind the way it was, wire just wasn't possible.

The transmitter warmed, Storch looked to Candido.

"Any time," Candido said, and turned to the periscope.
After a moment, the canister exploded.

The canister's side burst, but the blast's main force was
upward. They'd planned on that. It was a sudden belch of
light—a jet of incandescence streaking up, stabbing into
the sphere like a knife blade. A boll of smoke followed it
upward, more slowly. The sphere swallowed them, one
and then the other.

Candido watched. The sphere didn't change. The wind
blew unslackened. Candido shrugged. If a blast had been
going to do it, that blast would have done it. It hadn't.
This is the way the world ends, he thought, and wondered
where he'd heard the phrase. He turned the tank broadside to the wind—started the long, gradual descent down
the east slope of Gunbarrel Hill. After a while, he cut off
the supercharger and ripped the breather mask from his
face.

"Now what?" he asked.

All that came from L'Heuroux was silence. The wind
keened.

It was raining in Boulder again. The city's storm drains
had not been built for such downpours. Streets in the
lower sections were flooded. The creek was over its
banks, and up in the canyon a lot of private bridges were
gone. A house up there had been smashed by floodwaters,
and three people were missing. The State Police had a
six-year-old boy who'd been found, crying, climbing the
canyon wall in the rain. No one knew where he came
from. They couldn't get him to say much, and they
couldn't make much sense out of what he did say.

"The more I think about it," Candido said, "the more I
start wondering what made you think a blast would do it.
What's different about a blast from the way the wind's
tearing in there?"

Outside, through the window, he could see the trees writhe and sway in the rain like a modern dance group communicating agony. L'Heuroux cleaned his glasses with a rumpled handkerchief, not watching his hands.

"But remember," the physicist said, "we are dealing with a condition that is self-reinforcing. The wind that is entering the congruency is obviously part of the system. It seemed probable, therefore, that by disrupting the pattern of the winds, we could hope to destroy the condition."

"Well, it didn't work," Candido said.

L'Heuroux looked unhappy. "There was only one way we could find out."

At the end of the table, Trask harumphed. "I don't think that is advancing matters, gentlemen," he said. "I asked you here to discuss what action we will take now. All of us were disappointed when our attempt with explosives failed. We don't need to dwell on that aspect. I presume, Dr. L'Heuroux, you have new measures to propose."

"Of course," L'Heuroux said. Candido smiled grimly. If you could look inside the man's head, you'd probably see the wheels spinning like a one-arm bandit's. Thirty seconds, mister, or back you go to chasing neutrinos, or whatever it is physicists chase these days.

"Our first attempt," L'Heuroux said, "was to disrupt the condition which maintains the congruency by creating a violent disturbance in the material passing through into the congruency." He sounded like he was lecturing in a classroom—only natural, Candido thought, this being a classroom generously loaned by the university. "It was a logical thing to try first; however, it did not work. I think next we should try . . ." He paused, as if for dramatic effect.

"Yeah?" Candido asked.

"Next," L'Heuroux said, just as if Candido hadn't prompted him—except he bore down more heavily on the word than the word warranted—"we should test the condition's sensitivity to intense electromagnetic radiation. We have a laser which can supply the necessary output. And we have a million-gauss magnet. We should try that, also."

"Any special reason you think these'll do it?" Candido asked.

"Certainly," L'Heuroux said, as if a question like that could come only from a mentally deficient five-year-old. "We don't know enough about the congruency condition to be sure what type of external forces or fields it may be sensitive to. Therefore, what we must do is to investigate the condition's reaction to all the influences we can bring to bear."

"Translated into English," Candido said, "you're saying try anything, and if it doesn't work try something else." He tried to remember how many things Edison tried before he found something to make an electric light with. Two thousand? Four thousand? Fifteen? "All right, you've got a couple of things you want to try. If they don't do the job, what's next on your list?"

"Have you an alternative to suggest?" Trask asked.

"Me? I'm not educated the way this guy is," Candido said. "All I've got is a bachelor's in business administration. I don't know about this thing we're working on—I don't think he does, either, but I admit it. All I am, is an errand boy. Tell me the job and I'll do it, but now and then I like getting results from my work."

"I think," Trask said, "we'll try the laser and the magnet. Do you agree?"

Candido shrugged. "It beats thumb twiddling."

"We have to try everything possible," L'Heuroux said.

Candido wondered how you went about learning to breathe vacuum. It might come to that.

The wind still slammed across Gunbarrel Hill, and its cry was the cry of a slavering beast. The congruency's globe hovered like a ceaselessly spinning, pupil-less eyeball over the foundations of the laboratory it had destroyed.

If the laser made a sound, it wasn't sound that could be heard above the sheeting of the wind. The thing was mounted in the turret, to beam its pulses of light through the aperture left when the cannon was removed. All through the drive from Boulder, L'Heuroux had been pouring liquid nitrogen from a Dewar flask into the laser's reservoir. It made the interior of the tank very cold. The laser looked like a large, old-fashioned slide projector— an unlovely, functional piece of hardware. L'Heuroux fumbled with it. A blast of wind shook the tank. Something vibrated. A flash of white light filled the tank's interior. L'Heuroux muttered something in annoyed tones. He poured more nitrogen into the reservoir.

There were several more of the white flashes. Then the laser was working. L'Heuroux uttered a satisfied sound. Through the periscope, Candido saw momentary flickerings of red in the streaked, swirling dust clouds. They seemed to be on target, but it was hard to be sure. The tank was a hundred yards from the congruency, halted, with brakes on, tail to the wind and turret turned to aim the laser into the sphere. If the laser was on target, it wasn't doing any good. The sphere didn't change. The wind kept on blowing.

"Want to move up closer?" Candido asked. It was hard to talk clearly through his breather mask. The laser began flashing white again.

"It's heated up," L'Heuroux said. His voice was muffled. He gave the laser another jolt of nitrogen.

"We'll move closer," Candido said. It was possible, with all that dust and cloud in the air, that the laser's beams weren't getting through. He slipped the brakes, turned the tank toward the sphere, pushed up the throttle. He closed the distance to fifty yards, turned the tank butt to the wind. Ken Storch helped the physicist aim the turret again. The turret handled badly, pounded by the wind.

The laser flashed white only once this time, and then again Candido saw the flick of red in the airborne dust. This time, there was no question about its reaching the sphere. He could see the momentary stab of red in the swirling clouds inside the sphere. After a dozen pulses, the laser started flashing white again.

"Well, now we know two things that don't work," Candido said. He made sure the Diesel was behaving. Its reply was a snarling roar. He let go the brakes and moved the tank carefully toward the sphere. The wrecked foundation didn't make as much trouble this time. He knew the way, and the tank had bent or snapped off some of the steel rods the last time it was here. He stopped the tank, as before, in the zone of calm over which the sphere hung suspended like a shelter.

"All yours, Ken."

They'd rebuilt the handling rig for its new job. This time, instead of setting a massive canister down, it was to remove a small electromagnet from its supercooling bath and raise it close to the sphere. And this time—because it was a magnet—they couldn't use steel.

Storch manipulated the rig. The lid on the cold bath clattered aside and the magnet rose on the end of a double-jackknifed boom. The boom unfolded—extended to its full length like a scorpion's tail, stinger-tipped. Then the boom lifted—floated upward as if it weighed less than nothing. It stopped with the stinger only inches from the whirling tumult inside the sphere. Wisps of frosty air trickled upward like smoke from the magnet into the sphere.

"Any time you want," Candido said over his shoulder. "It's ready."

"I can see for myself," L'Heuroux said, peering through his view slit. There was the sound of him fiddling with equipment. "Ready?" he asked.

"All your show," Candido said. He watched the end of the boom—they were all watching. L'Heuroux closed the switch.

The boom whipped like a fishing rod struck by a big one. It bent down as if a powerful weight suddenly was hung on its end; Candido hadn't thought the aluminum alloy could bend so far without snapping. Then the current cut off automatically. The boom sprang upward. The tank jolted. The end of the boom—magnet and all—went into the sphere and . . .

JEHOSAPHAT!

The boom recoiled, and the magnet and the end of the boom were gone. All of the part that went into the sphere had vanished, as if jaws had chopped it off with the casual ease of a cow eating grass. Beside him, Storch uttered a yelp of surprise.

That's the last time I stick my head in *that* lion's mouth. It was a silly time to think of an old gag like that, but Candido thought of it. For maybe thirty seconds he couldn't think of anything else.

"Now we know three things that don't work," he said finally and put the tank into gear. "What's next?"

He got no answer all through the long descent down the eastern slope of the hill, nor during the long circle back westward, back to Boulder.

Two days later, the tank again snarled its way up the western slope of Gunbarrel Hill. The asphalt was smashed and broken from the previous times the tank had used these roads. Now and then, Candido noticed a chunk of rubble caught in a hollow where the wind couldn't sweep it away. Except for such as those, the roadway was clean.

The original handling rig had been put back on, and the new load weighed approximately one and a quarter tons. At first, Candido had balked at having anything to do with a chunk of condensed hell like this. One of the problems when they were inventing thermonuclear weapons had been that even a sophisticated implosion-type A-bomb like the Alamogordo and Nagasaki blasts could not produce a temperature hot enough to make heavy hydrogen touch off in a fusion chain reaction; so the ingenious and dedicated young men who are doing so much in this day and age to insure that men will all live as brothers—if they live at all—produced a special design of plutonium bomb that exploded, not as a simple, symmetrical fireball, but as a jet of plasma. Thus, instead of dissipating its thermal energy in an expanding sphere which, within two or three seconds, has become more than half a mile across—so diffuse it can no longer maintain its chain reaction—this detonator type of bomb concentrates its energy in the jet, exactly like a shaped charge of a more conventional explosive. The temperature thus obtained is on the order of ninety million degrees Centigrade—considerably hotter than the core of our sun—and quite sufficient to ignite an even more hellish chain reaction in any deuterium that happens to be in its path.

Very earnestly and soberly, they had emphasized to Candido that this was just the detonator part. They'd cannibalized a Titan missile—one of the thirty or forty that crouched in silos in a circle around Denver—but they'd left off the lithium deuteride part from the thing they entrusted to the tank's handling rig. The idea was to flood the entire volume occupied by the congruency with highly ionized nuclei of high kinetic energy, they said. The plutonium detonator was enough to do this. They thought there was a good chance this would disrupt the condition that maintained the congruency.

Candido wasn't impressed. They just wanted to try it because if they didn't they'd never be sure it wouldn't work. When he was a kid, he'd learned not to play with matches. They hadn't.

But the wind still blew, the floods in Boulder got worse, and no one had a better idea. They worked to convince him that the fail-safe mechanisms would prevent the bomb from going up until they were ready to set it off, and they promised him another hundred thousand. They put it in writing. He made sure his insurance was paid up, and said, "All right." He still didn't like that thing from a nose cone on the tank's front end, but he did like that extra hundred thousand.

"If this doesn't do it, I don't think anything will," he said. The roads were roads he'd traveled before—familiar. The force, and the gusty blasting, and the abrasive, high-sustained yell of the wind were like an incredible symphony by a modern composer, but a thing he knew so well he paid it no attention. He guided the tank, and when they got close enough he put on his breather mask and gave the others time to get their masks on, and then he turned up the supercharger and they went on all the way to the heart of the whirlwind, into the zone of calm. There was some new litter gathered under the sphere, but nothing of any great size or anything that would make any trouble. Even the roundabout path across the pier- and bar-studded foundation was easier. A beaten path.

And all the time he was thinking that the only men who could understand the congruency—what had created it and how it was maintained and how it could be erased— had vanished in the instant they made it, and L'Heuroux and all the other men who were trying to devise a weapon against it were fumbling children poking sticks into quicksand. Himself among them.

Ken Storch worked the handling rig with an expertise and care even greater than before—respect, Candido judged, for the power of the thing he was handling. This was something you could understand only by knowing that no sane imagination can really encompass the concept of twenty thousand tons of TNT. Storch was working the rig with the knowledge that its burden was a kind of death so blazing and immediate that even the fact of death would not have time to drive itself into his consciousness before his consciousness was shattered into its component atoms.

The arms of the handling rig withdrew from the bomb, and the bomb crouched squatly on a surface of crushed midden. All of its essential structure was concealed by its casing: they'd insisted on that—even if he were cleared to obtain such knowledge, they said, he had no need to know how it was put together. As if he could understand what he saw if he saw it. As soon as the arms were clear, he backed the tank away. In half an hour, the timing mechanism would arm the bomb—or if that failed, would at least release another mechanism so that a radio signal could arm it—and he intended to be far away from ground zero when it happened.

A tank didn't move very fast.

The bomb wasn't exploded until after they got back to Boulder. Candido and L'Heuroux and Ken Storch were permitted to stand under the rooftop portico of an ornate building while a few yards away in the same shelter a half-dozen men worked to ready the detonating equipment.

It was a lot more sophisticated than the radio they'd used in the tank on their earlier try. This equipment transmitted a beamed, highly intricate, frequency-modulated signal; it was only to that exact signal and no other that the bomb would detonate. A small transmitter in the bomb itself had been announcing that it had armed itself—that it waited only for the signal to turn itself into a small, vest-pocket edition of doomsday. The men had been working all morning, preparing to transmit the signal that would do it. They weren't ready yet.

Then, finally, they were ready. In spite of the rain and clouds that made it impossible to see even a quarter mile, Trask passed each of them a pair of smoked glasses and advised them not to look in the direction of the whirlwind's center. Somebody with a parade-ground voice began announcing a countdown.

Candido held the glasses in his hand, then thought better of it and put them on. Always take the advice of someone who knows more about a thing than you do. The countdown paced off the seconds to zero, and someone at the transmitter did something—Candido didn't see what because he was looking northward, toward the center of the whirlwind, nine miles away. He knew someone did something because the sky's gray drabness, dimly seen through the glasses, brightened momentarily like a flashbulb silently bursting its light in a smoke-thickened room. Then it was dark again. After a long time, thunder came.

Candido took off his glasses. The wind was still blowing. Rain still drilled the rooftop in endless, spattering patterns. He cast a skeptical glance at L'Heuroux.

The physicist shook his head. "At this point, it's impossible to say. We have a powerful storm system here. It will take several hours, at least, to dissipate."

"Then we'll wait," Candido said.

An hour later, the rain was still falling. And two hours later. Three, and the wind blew gusts as strong as ever. All night it stormed. In the morning, the creek's floodwaters had spread to even higher ground. Still the rain came down, and the wind drove smashing waves against the walls of buildings on the flooded land.

Candido lighted his pipe, bent the match double, and—not finding an ashtray in reach—stuck the match in his jacket pocket. They were back in the classroom again, and scrawled on the blackboard was a phrase: *Our daily life, which is all we have.* It was an annoying thing to have to look at, but his chair at the table was faced that way, so he couldn't turn aside. Nor could he change to another chair. Outside, as endlessly as a waterfall, the rain splashed down.

"Can you suggest anything at all?" Trask asked.

L'Heuroux rubbed a knuckle against his nose. "It's proving more refractory than we anticipated. Before we can recommend another approach, we'll have to study the data. I've gathered considerable information during our excursions. When we've analyzed this data, we'll know considerably more about this condition. Then we should be able to define a method of terminating it."

"What you're saying," Candido said, "is you don't know how to stop it."

L'Heuroux gave him an annoyed glance. "For the present, I must admit you are right. However, this is only a temporary state of affairs."

"Lasting," Candido said, "until we don't have any air left." There'd been a call last night. A small well in Kansas had blown and caught fire. He'd packed up his crew—all but Storch—and sent them east to fight it; they weren't needed here. But it was bad business to send them on a job and not go himself; if he didn't at least show on the scene of a job, somebody might get the hunch any man could do that kind of work—well, they could, if they learned all the tricks and had the nerve and more than a man's share of luck. If he let the crew go on too many jobs by themselves, some day there'd be three or a dozen guys in the business. One or two might even be rough competition, once they got themselves known. This job here was using up a lot of time. More than he'd expected, and no end in sight.

"I've got work waiting, other places," he said.

"We have you on retainer, I believe," Trask said.

"Yeah, you do," Candido said. "But I don't think you'll need me for the next forty-eight hours. Unless you've got an operation planned, I'm taking off."

"I believe you don't realize," Trask said, "this is something more than just another job. Unless this thing is stopped, no other work in the world will be worth doing. It's . . . why, it's the air we breathe!"

Candido had other things to do than twiddle his thumbs. "If you've got work for me, I'm here to do it. If you don't, it doesn't matter where I am. You'll know where to find me. I've got your retainer, and I'm on call twenty-four hours a day." He shoved his chair back, preparatory to leaving.

"Dr. L'Heuroux?" Trask asked.

"We'll have to study our data," the physicist said.

Candido rose, nodded to Trask, and turned to leave. He wondered how far his three hundred thousand would go toward building him a home-size, self-sufficient pressure chamber. Maybe he ought to set up a new business, too, selling air by the bottle—delivered to your door like a milkman—to the other people who built themselves pressure chambers. Yeah, he thought sourly—and maybe sell cans of vacuum to companies that made radio tubes. It made as much sense. Maybe . . .

At the door, he turned and came back. "How much is it worth if I stop this thing?"

Trask looked up, startled, like a deacon caught reading *Playboy*. "You have your retainer," he said stiffly.

"That's for doing the work," Candido said. "Pulling chestnuts and such. What I'm talking about now is figuring out how to do it."

Trask was suddenly quite interested. "Do you know how?"

"He can't possibly," L'Heuroux said. "He has absolutely no grasp of the principles involved."

"I know how," Candido said. He went around to the window, glanced out at the rain, the wind-wracked trees, and turned and leaned a shoulder against the window's frame. "It just came to me. Your trouble, you've been going at it wrong—like the mathematician when they handed him the one about how many flies in a bottle."

"I don't know what you're talking about."

Candido shrugged. "It's an old trick-type puzzle. You've got a bottle—say five-gallon size—with a fly in it. And you put another fly in it, and then a second later you put two more flies in, and another second later you put in four flies, and then eight, and so on."

L'Heuroux seized a stick of chalk—scrawled a formula on the blackboard under the phrase about our daily life. "Geometric progression. Yes, go on."

"Well, you keep at it," Candido said. "And after three minutes the bottle's exactly full. None left over. All right . . ."

L'Heuroux was scrawling hastily on the board. "What volume does a fly take up?"

"A third of a cubic centimeter," Candido said, and smiled as the physicist went into a frenzy of conversion formulae. "Now, what I want to know is, how full is the bottle at two minutes and fifty-nine seconds?"

The physicist worked quickly. His equations proliferated like ivy vines at east coast universities. Candido let him go on for almost a full minute. "That's enough," he said.

L'Heuroux turned. "Either the flies take up less space," he said, "or the bottle's larger. Considerably larger."

"I was just fudging the figures," Candido said. "They don't matter. You've been going at it wrong, just like I said you were. What the guy with the bottle's been doing is doubling how many flies he's got every time. Well, if that's what you're doing, and if you don't have any flies left over after you add the last batch, it figures the bottle was half full the time before."

"Well, of course," L'Heuroux said. "Why yes! Of course! But what does this have to do with the congruency?"

"Not a thing," Candido said. "I'm just saying that's how you've been going at it—hind end frontwards, and we say down in Texas that's not the recommended way to ride a horse." He shifted back to Trask. "You haven't said. What's it worth if I stop this thing?"

"Dr. L'Heuroux has been advising us as a public service," Trask said.

"He's been getting paid in feeling important," Candido said.

"I deny that!" L'Heuroux spluttered.

He didn't even know better than to interrupt a man who was haggling. Candido ignored the interruption. "From him you've been getting just about as much as you're paying for," he said. "I'll tell you what I want. I want a clear deed to that chunk of land. I want to own what's left after I've stopped it."

Trask looked like he'd been asked for an option on Brooklyn Bridge. "Is that all?"

"Any objections?" Candido asked.

"Oh no," Trask said quickly. "Yes—I'm sure it can be arranged. No trouble at all." He was so eager to make the deal he didn't think to ask what Candido wanted the property for. He was no businessman, Candido thought.

"Shake," Candido said, and stuck out his hand.

Three days later, they were ready. There was a steel mill and fabricating plant in Denver—not an especially big one, but big enough for the job. Mention that it was to fight the whirlwind was all the plant manager needed to schedule the project right away, and as soon as machinery and men were cleared of other jobs they went to work.

Candido went east to Kansas. He was gone only thirty-six hours. It was a routine job, and the fire snuffed at the first blast. He got back to Denver in time to catch four hours' sleep before the steel company phoned. His rig was ready.

He inspected the product and pronounced himself satisfied. It was fast, good work. He shook the plant manager's hand. This was a man who knew how to do business. The new equipment was loaded and trucked north to Boulder. They worked all night, and at ten in the morning the tank was ready to go.

It looked only a little like a tank now. More closely it resembled a beetle with a domelike shell steeply canted on its back and paired grasshopper legs projecting their knees forward at about the angle flags are carried on parade. The tank itself was small under all that. He just hoped the wind wouldn't be too strong against it. He'd have to hold tail to the wind all the way in. He hoped the Diesel would have power enough to drive the rig when they got there.

"Might as well start," he told Storch. He nodded to L'Heuroux. "Come along. You'll see the way to do it."

Proudly, L'Heuroux declined. Candido and Storch were alone in the tank when it left Boulder, groaning under its load. It was hard going. The wind drummed on the carapace, and though its round surface was like a shield to the wind, it was like a sail also, forcing the tank headlong forward. He'd had to plan out the way they would go, studying large-scale topographic maps until his eyes burned. He had to know that nowhere ahead was there too steep a slope, too sharp a declivity, or any obstacle the tank couldn't clear, for, once he began to move with this load, he was committed and could not turn aside. To let the wind gets its teeth around the edge of the carapace would be disaster. The tank would be thrown like a tumbleweed, wrecked, and they'd be helpless in that hurricane wind.

The rain-sodden earth bogged under the treads, but the wind kept the tank moving. Candido kept an eye on the pennon he'd fixed to the tank's prow, showing him the bearing of the wind. He kept the pennon whipping straight ahead. He had a quadrangle map taped to the panel in front of him. The route he'd planned was traced on it boldly. He watched for landmarks. The wind sang like a chorus in rage. The tank rocked and lurched and jolted. Blasts of wind shook it like a bone being gnawed.

The land was slopes and dells, and irrigation canals carved along the winding shoulders of low hills. Most of the canals were hardly more than ditches, easily crossed. One was a deep, slow river, full to its banks and flowing over. The bridge was where the map showed it, and wonder of wonders it held the tank's weight. He'd checked as much as he could, but the tank was a lot heavier than anything the bridge was built for. Until he was over, he hadn't been sure.

He'd started from Boulder almost straight east. The wind curved north and he turned with it. The tank crossed the southernmost extreme of Gunbarrel Hill and descended again to the plain beyond. Wire fences that had stood to the wind went down under the tank's weight. A cornfield, cut to stubs by the wind, streamed dust like the smoke of a brushfire. Wrecked foundations of barns and homes lay like open graves near the roads, now and then giving up another fragment to the tearing wind. The tank turned north and then westward, passed north of Gunbarrel Hill, and turned south again. The spiral was tighter now. Swinging east again, the tank mounted the hill's slope. The wind was like a powerful fist putting steady, driving pressure at the tank's rear. He should have given the tank some kind of an upward projecting spine, Candido thought, like a sailboat's jib, to help hold the thing butt to the wind. Too late to do it now. The tank crossed a small watercourse—dry now—bumping on the rocks and creaking with internal stresses.

They came to the crest. He could see the congruency's sphere off to his left, but he couldn't turn toward it. Keeping the wind behind him, he circled it widely. Then again, more closely. The foundation of the laboratory building was the final obstacle. For this and all its hazards there could be no evasion. The only way to go was straight in. The best he could do was possibly to sidle past the most forbidding obstructions. Candido studied the path ahead, trying to estimate the best possible path for the tank's treads. Bent stubs of steel bars gleaned rubbish from the wind like fangs raking flesh; they could as easily slash the tank's treads—break them. It was hard to make the brakes hold. He could hardly slow the tank's ponderous, headlong drive.

A thump and a lurch, and the tank mounted onto the platform. A crunch and a long, slowing grind as the tank straddled a pier and crumbled it under its belly. Candido felt something break. He wondered if it was part of the tank or the pier. The tank barged onward, bumping and lurching, and he had to work on the brakes to keep the tank square to the wind. Suddenly he felt something else give.

But the tank was in the dead zone now, under the sphere. The wind's seethe was like sawteeth, snarling, but now it was without force. Candido realized he hadn't put on his breather mask, and his ears felt plugged by the low pressure. With numb, fumbling, trembling fingers he got his mask on. He breathed deeply, only now aware how badly he needed it. His blood seemed to vibrate and burn.

He signaled to Storch, and the younger man unlocked and opened the turret-top hatch. Leaning far back, Candido could look up through the opening and see the sphere overhead, whirling like a model of the planet Jupiter. He shifted the tank back and forth, hitching it around until, finally, he was satisfied. The tank had to be in just the right position. Everything had to be just right. When he was satisfied, he put a hand on Storch's shoulder. He nodded.

"Ready," he said. The mask changed the word to a mumble, but Storch understood. The younger man checked the handling rig—modified again for this job—as carefully as if it were a supersonic aircraft. Only when he was satisfied did he put it in gear, to take power from the engine. Candido swung his periscope around to watch.

The hoodlike carapace separated into two hemispheres, like a beetle putting back its wing covers to fly. Fingertip-held between paired booms, the bowls turned upward and

extended like ladles, one to each side, as the booms
straightened out from their original hairpin bend. With a
hard snap, the booms locked straight, and the hemispheres—until now swinging free—locked level. Rigid,
Candido thought, and let himself breathe again.

Storch shifted to another gear. Slowly, for the hemispheres were heavy and the gears had been rigged to
account for that, the booms hinged upward. Candido
revved the Diesel. It changed the speed of the hemispheres' rising hardly at all. Minutes—it seemed like
days—passed. Candido thought grimly of the joke about
you'll never get it off the ground, and all he could hear
was the Diesel's growl and the cry of the wind and the
creak of metal joints under strain. The wind touched the
lips of the hemispheres. The tank vibrated. Something
buzzed resonantly.

Candido cracked the throttle full open. The engine
erupted. The hemispheres lifted like the wings of a
startled bird, and suddenly the wind caught them and
swung them upward in arcs on the ends of their booms.
The clang as they met overhead was like the gong of
doom. It burned the ears like dentists' drills.

Abruptly, wind battered the tank. Thunder drummed.
Candido's ears popped with a sudden jump of pressure.
The thunder boomed on and on, as if they were sealed in a
room with giants pounding on the walls. He could feel the
impact of the sound on his body. It was like being a child's
rag doll and being shaken. Slowly, by degrees, the
thunder died.

Candido took off his breather mask. Not needed now.
The air was full of dust. It smelled musty. Through the
open hatchway, he could see the steel globe enclosing the
space where the congruency had been—where it might
still be, for that matter, inside that steel container. He

breathed deeply. Not until now had he been sure the two hemispheres would meet and fit together without smashing each other, or without one or the other overshooting and passing into the congruency. But the engineers who'd worked on the thing had designed well. Neither had happened.

He climbed out of the tank. The wind still blew, but now it was only a gentle, warm wind. In all directions, storm clouds grayed the sky. As he stood there on the tank's superstructure, it began to rain. He got back inside. He closed the hatch against the torrent.

"We stopped it, Ken," he said. He opened the lunch pail he'd packed and handed a sandwich to Storch, took one himself, and poured himself a cup of coffee from the thermos. "The wind's still blowing out there," he said. "We'll have to stay here a while."

The jeep came, at last, in the last dim vestige of twilight. Its headlamps glistened on the wet concrete of the foundation, but the rain had stopped, finally, more than an hour ago.

By that time, Candido had been able to look the tank over. The treads had lost a total of seven shoes. Several more were badly torn. In two places, the linkage of the left tread was partly broken. A few more yards and likely the tank would have been immobilized. He felt numb and tight-skinned, thinking about that.

The congruency was still there, inside the steel shell. The hemispheres hadn't sealed perfectly, and a trickle of air was leaking in through the crack. Trask and L'Heuroux climbed out of the jeep and approached. Candido leaned against the tank and let them come. They picked their way across the hazards of the wrecked foundation with a flashlight, even so stumbling from time to time.

When they got there, at first they said nothing. Trask beamed the flashlight upward and played it over the steel globe's surface.

"I checked," Candido said. "No fractures. It'll hold, at least till we make a tighter one."

"Of course you realize," L'Heuroux said, "the congruency is still there, inside. This doesn't solve the problem."

"Doesn't it?" Candido asked. "Gentle breeze, we've got now." Actually, it was blowing a stiff twenty miles an hour, but the point was made. "When I've got a boat that leaks, I plug the hole."

The flashlight beam fixed on something that protruded from the globe's underside. It was a short length of pipe, with a valve wheel beside it. "What's that?" Trask asked.

"Just what it looks like," Candido said. "A storage tank's no good without an outlet."

"Outlet? Storage? I'm afraid I don't . . ."

"I'm starting a new business," Candido said. "That's why I wanted this chunk of land. I'm going to sell vacuums—the emptiest vacuums anywhere in the world. How much do you think they'll pay for a gallon of real nothing—no impurities?"

Another thought came. He smiled. Maybe he'd lay a pipeline—maybe all the way to the east coast. Plenty of people would pay for a vacuum you get just from turning a faucet, and he had an unlimited supply. Should be a real good business.

THE BROTHERHOOD
OF KEEPERS

PROLOGUE

The cold wind screamed and drove dart-chips of crystal stuff deep into Chier-cuala's fur.

Chier-cuala struggled up the hill. It was hard going. His walking flippers couldn't find good footing in the white, soft powder that smothered the land, and the slope was steep. His stubby legs ached with fatigue. He floundered and wallowed in the white powder. It was cold.

He couldn't remember any cold time like this one. Never had it been so cold. Never had the wind blown so hard, so endlessly. It had not stopped for many sleeping times. And never had the strange white powder lain so thick on the ground.

Chier-cuala couldn't understand.

The cold, hard darts of crystal stuff clung to his fur. He brushed them away. The wind plastered more against him. The wind leaked through his thick pelt and chilled him. His walking flippers ached and throbbed with the cold. He whimpered softly.

Stubbornly, he pressed on toward the crest of the hill. He needed food. His hunger was a compelling agony. It was the only thing that could have driven him out into this cold and wind. Always before, when a cold time came, he had huddled in his lair until it stopped—until the sky was blue again, and the powderlike white stuff on

135

the ground turned to wetness, and the air turned warm.

But this time the cold had not stopped, and the wind still blew, and the sky remained gray. He had not eaten since . . .

He remembered the last thing he ate—the small, clumsy creature he had caught in the recesses of his lair. It was so small he would have ignored it, except he was starved.

And after he ate it, he had slept through a dark time, and then there was a bright time during which he did not eat because there was nothing, and then another dark time through which his sleep was troubled by visions of edible creatures.

Now, forced out of his lair by his hunger, he climbed the hill. The odd creatures on the hilltop had given him good things to eat, sometimes, when he did things which they made him understand they wanted him to do. Purposeless things, and some of them were very hard, but the odd creatures gave him good things to eat when he did them.

The slope was covered with the cold, white powder, and the broken-off stems and stalks of what had been a forest stuck up nakedly. Shattered pieces of them, buried under the white powder, slashed his walking flippers and blue stains marked his path.

Chier-cuala tried to pull himself up the steep slope by grasping the upright stalks in his prehensile, paddlelike forepaws. The stalks broke. He fell back—rolled downhill in a whirl of the white powder. It got into his fur. It was wet and cold.

He lay where he stopped rolling. He whimpered, too weary to move. Finally, knowing he must move and making the effort, he struggled up and went on. He did not try to grasp the stalks again.

At last, he found a way to the hilltop. The wind blew

more fiercely up there. It slashed through his fur and chilled his body. He cried softly, miserably. His walking flippers were full of pain—turning numb. The blue stains in his footprints grew large. Clumsily, he stumbled across the hilltop toward the place of the odd creatures.

He whacked a forepaw against the flat thing that blocked the entrance. It did not move. He slapped again, and then again and again, harder and harder. He uttered a broken, heart-forsaken cry. He could not understand why the odd creatures did not take away the entrance block and give him food.

He had to have food. He was hungry.

The cold wind screamed.

Chier-cuala slapped the door and sobbed.

1

They called it coffee, even though it was brewed from the stems of a plant which originated forty light-years from Earth. It had a citric, quininelike taste. Hot and sweetened, it served the same function as coffee. Some people even preferred it.

It was an odd hour; Sigurd Muller and Lewis Tedesco were alone in the commissary. Muller sipped from his cup—it was still too hot. He set it down.

"What do you think about it?" he asked the younger man.

Tedesco made an awkward, unconvincing shrug. "It sort of scares me," he admitted.

"Yeah?" Muller leaned his weight on the table. "Why?"

The young man was embarrassed. "Well," he explained, "you remember last year, just after I got here, you put me through the test sequence—the same one you use on the floppers?"

Muller smiled. "I put all you young squirts through it. You're supposed to be smart, or you wouldn't get to come here. It's a good calibration standard."

Tedesco nodded. "I didn't do so good," he said.

"You did average," Muller recalled, as if it was an unimportant matter. He tapped a fingernail on the table top. "The trick with an intelligence test, you've got to make it tougher than the smartest guy to take it. Otherwise, it's a no-good test." He slouched back and half closed his eyes. "In the seven years I've been here, the average intelligence of scientist-candidates hasn't gone up an inch. I guess you kids have reached an evolutionary plateau."

"That's the thing that scares me," Tedesco confessed. "I mean, I knew all about mazes and problems, but the set you've got had me stopped. And when I saw that flopper catch on to the pattern maze—when it didn't even know the principle of a maze . . ." He hesitated. "I'm scared," he repeated lamely.

"It was a smart one, all right," Muller said.

Tedesco wasn't ready to go quite that far. "It could have been a fluke," he suggested.

Muller shook his head. "No fluke," he said. He leaned closer. "What if I told you the one we had today wasn't the first?"

Tedesco frowned. "I hadn't heard of any others," he said doubtfully. "And I know there haven't been any since I've been here."

"You've just been here a year," Muller reminded him. "I had two the year before you came. They both came from the same place—the same place this one came from."

"Ziggurat Mountain?"

"Yeah," Muller said. "An enclave shut up in the mountains with no way out and a population of about seven and a half thousand. It used to be six thousand—it's been going up the last ten years."

Tedesco thought about that for a while. Idly, he turned the handle of his cup one way, then the other. "Just the sort of place we could expect it," he said finally.

Muller nodded, smiling. "Now tell me why."

"Well, it's a small population in a limited area—isolated—and they're under extreme selection pressure. It's the sort of situation that's almost sure to show an evolutionary trend."

"You got that out of Houterman's book," Muller said.

Tedesco flushed. "Sure. But he's right, isn't he?"

Muller shrugged. "It's the same basic principle," he agreed. "But he wasn't talking about the setup here. He was talking about evolution by genetic drift—where the genes already exist. That's not what's happening here."

"Are you sure?" Tedesco asked hesitantly.

"Yeah," Muller stated. "We've had this station here ever since the planet switched from Alpha to Beta—that's close to a thousand years. We've been testing floppers all that time. If the genes had been around back then, they'd have shown up in the first couple of centuries. They didn't. The first time a flopper showed up even halfway intelligent—don't scowl like that, I've checked the records—was just forty years ago. And guess where he came from."

"Ziggurat Mountain?" Tedesco guessed.

Muller rapped a fist on the table. "Right," he said through his teeth. "It's a mutation. It's got to be. And it happened right there in the enclave."

Tedesco was silent a moment. "Why did you kill it?" he asked.

"Same reason I killed the other two," Muller said. "I

want a look at its brain. The first two—I thought they were flukes. Now I don't think so—and a look at this one's brain cells will prove it."

"But wasn't that against the rules?" Tedesco wondered. "I mean, a flopper showing exceptional characteristics . . ."

Muller scratched his beard. "So it was against the rules," he said. "I had to find out, and that's the only way."

Abruptly, then, he changed the subject—or seemed to. "You go back with the supply ship, don't you?"

It wasn't really much of a question. Only a very unusual scientist-candidate stayed more than one year. Tedesco nodded.

Muller smiled, satisfied. "O.K.," he said. "When you get back, you can talk about this all you want. But while you're still here . . . it didn't happen. None of it. Understand?"

"I . . . I think so," Tedesco said slowly. "But . . . why?"

"Because they're getting smart," Muller told him. "If we don't do something, they'll all get smart—smarter than we are. And they're vicious—you've seen what the wild ones are like. Well, we can't let it happen. That's why we've had this station here all these years—to watch 'em, because someone way back then figured this might happen. So we can stop 'em if it does. But there's just enough softheads around here that *want* it to happen. We don't want them finding out—or anybody else."

"Oh," Tedesco said. He frowned helplessly. "But what can we do? How can we stop them?"

"Don't ask." Muller chuckled. "I might tell you."

"Well, I'd like to know," Tedesco said.

Muller leaned his weight on the table. He tapped the

hard surface confidentially. "You heard who's coming in the supply ship this time?"

Tedesco paused, trying to remember. "Well, there's Blackett, and Holman, and . . ."

Muller waved a hand. "I don't mean personnel. I mean just for a look around."

"Hitchcock?" Tedesco wondered incredulously. "But he's . . . he'd be on *their* side. He always is."

"He might be," Muller admitted, "if he knew what he was doing. Most of the time, he just meddles. That's what he's going to do here."

"Are you sure?"

"Yeah. I'm sure," Muller said, smiling. "I'm going to help him." He laughed.

"I was horrified, gentlemen. Horrified."

That, Adam Hitchcock decided, was the thing to say about Xi Scorpii when he got back to Earth. That was what he would tell his Society for Humane Practices, to signal the beginning of a new crusade.

The Xi Scorpii Foundation would protest, of course. They would say he was misrepresenting the facts. But that didn't worry him. Men always said that when he exposed their iniquities, and it never made the slightest difference. The public always recognized the truth.

Hitchcock made his decision as soon as he arrived at Xi Scorpii—while he was still descending the stairway scaffold that huddled close up against the *Wayfarer*'s flank. His mood was surly—it had been a bad trip out. The *Wayfarer* was a cargo ship, with only minimal provision for passengers; he had been obliged to share his cabin with a young scientist-candidate whose single-minded enthusiasm for the mutational aspects of genetic chemistry left him with a very unflattering picture of the scientific mind.

Carrying a piece of luggage in each hand, Hitchcock trudged down the stairs. It was a long way down, and the scaffold felt rickety. It trembled and creaked in the wind. Any civilized place would have had an elevator. The wind was cold. It howled around him. It chilled his throat. It penetrated through the thin overcoat he wore—a coat which was all he'd have needed on any civilized planet. His ash-gray hair was tangled. His ears tingled painfully. His jowls were numb. His head ached and his nostrils watered. It was a dreadful planet.

He paused on the stairway and set down his bags. He tried to draw his collar tight. It was no use—the cold air continued to ooze through. Grimly, he stared down again. The camera looped over his shoulder bumped his side.

The landing field toward which he descended was too small and too ill-kept for anything but a survey camp. It was nothing but a leveled-off rock plain without pavement, no larger than a city block. Various atmosphere craft crowded the edge of the field on the side nearest the outpost's black dome. On the other side, a cold sea spread all the way to the edge of the sky. Sluggish, floe-chocked waves smashed on the rocks, building castles of ice with their spray.

Critically, Hitchcock glanced toward the bright sun. It burned in a blue, clear sky, but it gave no warmth. Nor was the system's other star more than a fleck of light down close to the ice-dappled sea.

Definitely, this planet wasn't fit for anything to live on—neither man nor any other creature.

Already, he saw as he continued his descent, the ship was disgorging its cargo. Its hoist settled massive crates and bundles of supplies on sledges which were dragged toward the dome by harnessed teams of shaggy, dirty-white, short-legged creatures about the size of very large dogs. At rest, while waiting for their sleds to be loaded, they squatted on their hind legs, their apparently boneless arms curled up almost double and their mittenlike paws pressed flat against their bodies. No one was directing them. They seemed to know what to do.

Halfway down the scaffold, Hitchcock stopped again. He turned to the man behind him and pointed at the laboring creatures. "Are those the natives?" he asked. He had to shout to be heard above the howl of the wind.

The man—another of those eager young scientist-candidates—didn't seem to understand the question. "The floppers?" he wondered uncertainly, then nodded.

Hitchcock unlimbered his camera and put the scene on tape. It was an outrage! The poor things were slaves! When he reached the bottom, a man in a thick, hooded garment was waiting beside a sled with removable benches set on it. Its eight-flopper team squatted stoically, cringing from the frigid wind. The man reached out to take Hitchcock's luggage. "Climb aboard," he invited loudly. "We'll be heading for the dome in a minute, as soon as the rest of you get down."

Hitchcock didn't let go of his bags. He glanced at the harnessed floppers. "Thank you," he said stiffly—and his teeth rattled with the cold. "I prefer to walk."

The man shrugged, but he looked concerned. "It's a long way to hike in this wind," he advised, nodding toward the dome a half mile away. "The first thing you know, you've took a deep breath, and then you've got frost in your lungs. Better ride along with the rest of us peasants."

"If they have to pull me, I will not ride," Hitchcock insisted.

"Who—the floppers?" The man was incredulous. "They grew up in this weather. They eat it for breakfast."

"They didn't grow up to be slaves," Hitchcock said.

The man looked at him queerly. "You must be this

Hitchcock we heard about," he said. "Listen, mister—
somewhere you've got the idea these floppers are people.
They're not. They're just smart animals."

"No creature in the universe was ever born to be a
slave," Hitchcock said.

The man made an exasperated noise. "Just take my
word for it. If you walk, you'll wish you hadn't. Now
climb aboard. We're ready to move."

He jerked an imperative thumb at the sled. Hitchcock
eyed him for a long, stubborn moment.

Then the cold and the wind persuaded him. He went to
the rear of the sled and put his baggage in the rack, all the
time stamping his feet to put warmth in them. His hands
were numb and blue. Shivering, he told himself that the
creatures could endure the climate better than he could,
and that they would drag the sled whether he rode it or
not. He would not add much to their burden.

But he hadn't forgotten his mission. He raised his
camera and taped the scene—first the sled and its load of
huddled, wind-lashed passengers, then swung the lens
forward to the floppers waiting mutely in their harness.
They had a sad, downtrodden look. Hitchcock let his
camera dwell on them.

Unfortunately, they were ugly as sin.

He demanded quarters of his own and got them. Coldly,
he rejected the suggestion that a flopper could carry his
luggage. Lordlike, austere, he strode along the corridor to
his room.

When he found it, a flopper was inside. With single-
minded concentration, it went on sweeping while Hitchcock laid his bags on the bed. For all the sign it gave, it
might not have noticed his entrance.

It would have been as tall as Hitchcock, but its legs
were too short. Its pelt was silvery gray. Its head was

revolting—a slab-shaped, almost neckless thing set on top of a shoulderless body. The big, goggling eyes were placed far apart, leaving space between them for the vertical slit of the lipless mandible-jaws and the muscles that powered those jaws. On top, the single ear stood up like the peak of a much-too-small cowl.

The rest of the creature was equally hideous—the flexible arms as seemingly boneless as a fire hose, and the flat, big, floppy feet. It was marsupial, with a pendulous pouch that pulsed spasmodically, as if something alive was inside. But the creature was also unquestionably— almost indecently—masculine. It had a musky smell. Hitchcock stared at it with sick distaste.

It continued to work the broom with brainless absorption. It swept around Hitchcock's feet as if he was a piece of furniture.

"Stop that!" Hitchcock said. He backed away.

The flopper stopped. Looking up at him dumbly, it rolled its bulbous brown eyes.

"Get out of here!" Hitchcock told it.

The flopper just looked at him, dumb and trembling. Tentatively, it started sweeping again.

"No! Get out!" Hitchcock yelled.

Frantically, the flopper went on sweeping. It tried to work too fast. The broom flew out of its flipperlike hands and whacked Hitchcock's knee. Hitchcock yowled with pain and rage.

The creature fled, bounding out the door on all fours. Hitchcock grabbed the broom and chased it as far as the hall, until it disappeared around a corner.

Slamming the door, Hitchcock went back and sat on the bed. He rolled down his hose to inspect his whacked knee. It was an angry red, but not damaged.

The stupid brute!

Someone knocked on the door. Hitchcock pulled up the

hose and refastened the top to his undershorts. Smoothing down his tunic skirt, he said, "You may enter."

A slovenly dressed man came in—ankle socks, ill-fitting kilt, and turtleneck. He had a full, untrimmed, black beard. "What's the ruckus in here?" he asked.

"Ruckus?" Hitchcock repeated innocently. "Here?"

"Yeah. Here," the man insisted. "One of my cleaning boys skedaddled out of this hallway and dove in his hutch like a carload of hell was looking for him. He'd cleaned up this far, so he must've been here." He glanced down at his feet. "That's his broom." He picked it up.

"I told it to leave," Hitchcock said. "I refuse to be a party to its slavery."

"Exactly how did you say it?" the man asked.

"I asked it please to get out of here," Hitchcock stated primly. "I must say the creature was unpardonably stupid. I had to repeat it twice."

The bearded man looked skeptical, but he didn't challenge the assertion. "That's not in his vocabulary," he told Hitchcock. "You're new here, so I guess it isn't your fault. But after this, if you want a flopper to scram, say, 'That's all,' and he'll get right out. They're real obedient if you're proper with 'em. But you got to give 'em the right commands."

"I'll keep my own room clean," Hitchcock said frigidly. "Keep your slaves out of here."

"If you want 'em to stay out, bolt the door," the bearded man advised. "It'll worry the boy to have his routine monkeyed with, but it's better than to scuttle his training."

"Keep them away from me," Hitchcock repeated.

The man looked him up and down. His eyes were steady. "Don't expect 'em to understand everything you say," he said finally. "They don't."

He backed out of the room and shut the door.

Mindful of his banged knee, still seething, Hitchcock rummaged in his bags for the liniment tube he always carried. He most certainly *would* keep his door locked. The mere thought of that mindless creature pawing his possessions made him tremble with rage.

It was terrible, the indignities a man of good will was forced to endure!

2

"I hope your room is satisfactory," Ben Reese said as they began Hitchcock's tour of the outpost. He was a plump man, Ben Reese—almost forty, with a round face and an almost bald scalp. Hitchcock worried him.

"Adequate," Hitchcock replied. He had a nerve-rattling way of walking—never looking where they went. Constantly, he twisted his head first in one direction, then another. "Spartan, but adequate."

"We don't have many luxuries here," Reese admitted. "Everything we have has to come in the supply ship."

"Um-m-m," Hitchcock muttered. "Tell me, Mr. Reese, what is it like to be the undisputed monarch of an entire solar system?"

Shocked speechless, Reese stopped in his tracks and stared at the man. "I don't think you understand," he said finally. Hitchcock walked loftily on. Reese had to run to catch up. "All I do is . . . is coordinate our research work here," he explained, breathless. "And . . . and I estimate our supply needs. The ship only comes once a year— someone has to do it."

But Hitchcock's attention was on something else. Maybe he was deaf—he didn't seem to have heard.

They followed the dome's main hall. Their buskined feet whispered softly on the tiles. Only a few people passed them. In the dim light, the near silence, it was like the cellars under a castle. Floppers intent on their tasks scurried past like industrious gnomes.

At the hall's end, where it split into two out-curving corridors, Reese paused. "Would you rather see the anatomy lab first?" he asked. "Or the biochemical department?"

Hitchcock didn't reply. Not far up one of the corridors, a flopper was belaboring the floor with a mop. A sloppy bucket sloshed by its feet. With a barely perceptible look of glee, Hitchcock turned his camera on it.

The flopper worked on, oblivious of them. After a long moment, Hitchcock stopped his camera and turned. "You said something?" he inquired.

"I asked what you wanted to see first," Reese said.

Hitchcock glanced down at him as if he were a bug. "It makes absolutely no difference. Before I am done here, I will expect to have seen everything."

They went on with the tour. For Reese, it was an endless trial. Hitchcock listened only to the things he cared to hear and trained his camera on every laboring flopper they passed.

Reese endured it as long as he could. He had no illusions about why Hitchcock had come to Xi Scorpii— the man was convinced the floppers were victims of human oppression and planned to expose it. He and his Society for Humane Practices had already done something like that on a score of other worlds, completely disregarding the actual facts. Reese had hopes he could persuade the man to leave Xi Scorpii alone, but he had no idea how to do it.

Finally, when Hitchcock unlimbered his camera at the

sight of a flopper washing dishes in the commissary, he thought he saw his chance.

"Why are you doing that?" he demanded.

"I am gathering evidence," Hitchcock replied. He held his whirring camera steady, not looking at Reese. "When I return home, I intend to see this outrage stopped."

Reese was nonplused. Even knowing Hitchcock's intentions, he could not imagine what the man was talking about.

"I will not stand idle and see any person enslaved," Hitchcock said.

So that was it. "But . . . they're *animals*," Reese explained. "We've trained them to do these jobs because we don't have enough people here to do them. They . . . they're just domesticated animals."

Hitchcock put up his camera and turned. "Do you ask me to deny the evidence of my own eyes?" he demanded. "I see this one washing dishes, and you tell me it's only an animal?"

"Why not?" Reese wondered. "It's a . . . a rather intelligent animal, of course—somewhat more advanced than, say, the terrestrial chimpanzee. But that still leaves it far below the human level. Are . . . are you against using animals to take the burden of work off a man's shoulders?"

Hitchcock huffed. "Let us continue our tour."

He walked off, forcing Reese to tag after him. They were out in the corridor again when Hitchcock said, his voice scathing, "I was advised that the welfare of the natives was being neglected, but—"

"Who told you that?" Reese asked blankly.

Hitchcock was impatient. "It's common knowledge on every civilized planet," he said.

"But it . . . it's not true!" Reese protested. "You can't

even properly call them natives. They're only animals—in fact, rather primitive animals in most respects. They do have fairly well developed brains—that is, we can teach them some reasonably complicated things, and they have moderately good judgment—but they haven't any abstract reasoning power, or the ability to symbolize, or . . . or social instinct—none of the things that make people human."

"I came here," Hitchcock replied, "to judge that for myself. I have heard excuses like yours on other planets I've visited—planets where the most outrageous violations of decency were practiced. Why, can you imagine— on Epsilon Eridani people were actually *eating* them! As for conditions here, I will come to my own conclusions."

He paused then, slowed his stride, and turned to Reese. "Well, where do we go now?"

Originally, Reese had planned for them to continue along the corridor. The microfilm reference library would have been next. But now, suddenly, he changed his mind. He nodded across the corridor toward a spiral stairwell.

"Down there," he said.

As they clambered down the narrow stairs—Reese going first—Reese said, "So far, you've only seen floppers who were born here—I mean, here in the dome. You see, when this"—he gestured inclusively around—"was being built, they were brought in for study, to set a standard we could guide our work by. They've been here ever since. We've let them breed without any control, and they haven't been under the selection pressure the ones outside have been under, so they still ought to be almost identical to their ancestors. That makes them a good comparison standard against the floppers outside."

They emerged from the stairway into a corridor that looked very much like the one they'd left. Reese led Hitchcock into a side corridor which ended at a double-doored threshold. Passing through, they walked out onto a gallery overlooking a roomful of partitioned cubicles on the floor below. Most of the cubicles had floppers in them.

"These are wild floppers we've brought in to examine," Reese explained.

Hitchcock crossed to the rail and aimed his camera downward. "They are no different from the others," he said. "Must you keep them in solitary confinement? It's inhuman!"

"But it's not like that at all," Reese tried to explain. "They come from different geographical areas, and we put them back when we're done with them. We have to keep them apart to prevent them from breeding. Besides, they might kill each other."

The sound of their voices had made the floppers look upward. Their lipless, fleshless jawbones clashed. Hitchcock moved his camera back and forth across their upturned, bloodlusting faces.

"I want you to see something," Reese said. He crossed to a cold locker recessed in the wall and took out a large haunch of meat. It was a hideous blue-green color, and a translucent, cartilaginous length of bone protruded from it.

"Watch," he told Hitchcock.

Hitchcock was horrified. "You're going to feed them— *that?*" he demanded. "But it's putrescent!"

"Oh, no," Reese assured him, earnestly shaking his head. "That's its natural color." He did not add that it came from a domesticated flopper that had died; Hitchcock would have claimed he was promoting cannibalism. Crossing to the rail, he dropped the haunch into one of the pens.

The flopper grabbed it before it hit the floor—grabbed it between its flexible paws and crammed it against its maw. It masticated the meat, bone and all, with its toothless, bare-bone jaws. It worked the meat to a messy pulp and sucked it inward, its throat pulsing hideously.

When they saw the meat dropped, the floppers in the surrounding pens tried to get to it—tried to leap and climb out of their prisons, but the pen walls were too smooth and high. Blind-stubborn, they kept on trying, slamming their bodies again and again against the partitions. They yelped crazily. The room was full of thunder, rasping screams, and screechings.

Through it all, with wild looks of apprehension, the favored one suckled and gobbled at the haunch. Its lipless mouth worked greedily. Trickles of blue-stained drool oozed down its front. In a remarkably short time, the haunch was gone without a trace.

The other floppers were still trying to reach the pen where they had seen the haunch fall. And now, gorged and still drooling, the flopper in that pen was trying to get out, too. It leaped and fell back, leaped and fell back, time after time—its goggling brown eyes turned upward, its appetite whetted. Involuntarily, Hitchcock flinched back from its ferocity, then bent eagerly forward so his camera could witness its rage. The crazed creature's hacking cries were swallowed in the general tumult.

Hitchcock stopped his camera, finally, and turned. He shouted something. The noise smothered his words. Reese gestured to the door. He led Hitchcock outside.

When the door closed behind them, shutting off the ear-blasting noise, Hitchcock turned on Reese.

"They seem to hate you," he observed. "Don't you feed them?"

"We fed them not more than an hour ago," Reese said, with a glance at his watch. "They didn't behave with much intelligence, did they?"

"Hm-m-m," Hitchcock growled. "A starving man would act that way."

"But these . . . they weren't starved," Reese argued. "They were probably half-starved when they were captured, of course, but they've been fed since then—most of them several times."

"I cannot believe that," Hitchcock said. "Those creatures were *starved.*"

Reese shook his head. "Their reaction was pure habit," he said. "Food is scarce for them. It's been scarce all their lives. Their . . . their ravenousness is natural for them."

With a look of scornful pleasure on his face, Hitchcock pounced. "May I ask why you permit them to starve?"

It came to Reese that he had made a mistake. In trying to win a small argument, he had given Hitchcock support for a much more serious, much more difficult argument.

"Why . . . why," he stammered, "we're scientists. We're here to . . . to *study* the floppers. It's our whole reason for being here. You see . . . you see, we believe the floppers stand a very good chance of developing human-level intelligence. We've been watching for signs of it for nearly a thousand years, now. And if we tried to make their lives any easier, it would interfere with their development."

"Nonsense," Hitchcock sniffed.

"It isn't nonsense," Reese insisted. "It's a logical conclusion based on the principle of natural selection. If you'd let me explain the situation here—"

"I am fully aware of the situation here," Hitchcock replied. "I consider it disgraceful."

Reese gritted his teeth. "This is an unusual planet," he said earnestly, hoping the man would pause and begin to doubt. "That is, its orbit is unusual."

"Well, certainly," Hitchcock said. "I would expect a

planet in a double-star system to have a distorted orbit."

"It's worse than that," Reese persisted mildly. "When this system was explored the first time, this planet had an orbit around Alpha—it's still in the books as Alpha II. But now it's going around Beta."

"What?" Hitchcock boggled. "Preposterous."

"It's true," Reese said helplessly. "And not only that, we think Alpha and Beta have been passing it back and forth ever since it was formed. They have rather eccentric orbits around each other, you see, and they come rather close together every forty-five years. If the planet is in the right part of its orbit when they're closest together, the other star captures it."

"Does this happen very often?" Hitchcock asked sarcastically.

Reese made a helpless gesture. "It's different every time," he explained. "The planet might stay with one star for a hundred thousand years, or maybe just for a couple of hundred. Each time it's traded, it takes up a different orbit—that is, different from any it's ever had before. The next time it happens will be three and a half thousand years from now."

Hitchcock sniffed. "This is very interesting, if true," he said. "But it has nothing to do with the deplorable way you have treated the natives."

"It has everything to do with how we treat them," Reese insisted. "You see, every time the planet changed orbits, its climate has been drastically altered. We have a lot of geological evidence of that. I guess Alpha and Beta are more similar than most binary pairs, but there's still quite a difference in their radiation. And the various orbits the planet took put it at different distances out from them."

"I presume this has some significance," Hitchcock interrupted testily.

Reese nodded. "We're almost certain that the living things on this planet can endure great extremes of climate—if they couldn't, they'd have died out long ago. It's even possible that life here was wiped out completely by some of the changes—it might have happened hundreds of times before the cycle we're seeing now got started. I don't suppose we'll ever know for sure."

Hitchcock looked down at him with a fastidious expression on his face. "Never have I heard such a preposterous idea," he declared. "As if the spark of life could be snapped off and on like an electric lamp."

Reese had heard of people who thought like that, but he had never met one before. It was like meeting something out of the dark ages. "I was trying to emphasize how . . . how hardy the life forms on this planet must be," he explained diplomatically. "How . . . how *adaptable*. We think they have the capacity to evolve hundreds of times faster than the native life of any other world we know. So you see, being here is a wonderful opportunity to see evolution at work. And—"

"You have not yet explained," Hitchcock reminded him again, "why you have neglected the welfare of the natives here . . . why you vivisect them, and—"

So he was back where he started, Reese thought. It was discouraging. "Why, I thought it was obvious," he said. "The floppers aren't really intelligent—yet. But they do have the . . . the potential to *become* intelligent. It's really almost inevitable in a situation like this—that is, with an unpredictably erratic environment, intelligence is almost certain to develop sometime, because intelligence is the one specialization that gives an animal the ability to live in a whole lot of different environments. You see, we're not just studying the evolution process here—we're . . . we're watching the development of intellect. Sooner or later, somewhere on this planet, the floppers are

almost certain to become . . . to become *intelligent.* I
mean, intelligent the way a . . . a human being is
intelligent. And we want to be here. We want to see it
happen. We've never had the chance to see it happen in
an animal before."

Hitchcock scowled. "You speak as if men were animals," he said. "As if an animal could have a mind."

"Well, human beings are a form of animal," Reese put
in.

"That," Hitchcock snapped, "is nonsense. Dangerous
nonsense. I want to hear no more of it." He hitched up his
camera's shoulder strap. "As for this matter of intellect, I
have only your word they are not intelligent right now. I
will have to have proof, Mr. Reese. I must have proof."

Ben Reese gave up. He could not prove a thing to a man
who refused to believe.

INTERLUDE

*It was a good time to hunt. No wind blew loose snow on
the screecher's tracks, blotting them. No mistiness •ob-
scured the distance, and the sky's light shimmered on the
white land. Qua-orellee kept his eyes tightly lidded to
lessen the glare. The tracks were new. The beast could not
be very far ahead. Qua-orellee loped along, following
them, but he stayed well to one side of the trail for fear
the snow would open under him like a mouth and devour
him.*

*He had seen it happen, once. He and some others of the
hunting pack were following the tracks of a bushy-tailed
runner, and one of the people went close to the creature's
trail. A hole opened under him and he was gone. Qua-*

orellee and the others fled instantly. Since that time, Qua-orellee had never gone closer than three body-lengths to any creature's trail—not even his own.

The screecher's tracks vanished over the crest of a rise. Qua-orellee veered away from the trail, to reach the crest well away from where the screecher had been. It was hard to climb the slope with only his rear legs. He dropped down and hobbled along using one of his front limbs. In the flipperlike hand of the other, he clutched his rock.

His rock was a treasure—his only possession. He would need it when he came upon the screecher and had to kill it. It was hard to find a rock of a good shape and size for killing beasts with, but a rock was wonderfully better than ice. Ice broke easily. It didn't keep its shape. And, too, a person had to use a stronger blow to kill with it.

He never let the rock out of his sight, and rarely out of his hand. He clasped it to him when he slept, and he slept in his own secret place. Any other of the pack would eagerly kill him—if they dared to try—to possess that rock.

He topped the rise. Below him, the screecher's trail turned down along the valley, away from him. Qua-orellee let out a high-hacking cry, to tell the people who had joined him in the hunt that the screecher had turned in a new direction. Shrill, rasping calls came back from either side of him, repeating the news. Then another cry came from down valley—the beast had been seen.

Qua-orellee clutched his rock against him and plunged eagerly down the slope. His big flipper-feet and short legs made him stumble. He rolled all the way to the bottom in a cloud of snow, but he didn't let go of his rock. No matter what happened, he would never let go of his rock.

He stood up and shook the snow out of his fur. Up valley, two more of the pack—not encumbered with rocks—were bounding down the hillside on all fours.

They continued across the valley and up the other slope.
When they reached the crest, they headed toward where
the screecher had been seen. Qua-orellee *stayed in the*
trough of the valley. He followed the trail.

The valley curved around the bulk of a massive, steep
hill. As he rounded the turn, Qua-orellee *saw the*
screecher far ahead. Three people up on the ridge had got
abreast of the beast, and one of them was lolloping down
into the valley to head it off. On the ridge on the other side
of the valley, the two who had crossed over were rapidly
catching up, running on all fours. Qua-orellee *was far*
behind. He hurried as fast as he could on his short legs
and large feet.

The other pack-people closed down into the trough of
the valley, forming a wide-spaced crescent-circle line in
front of the screecher. They had picked up chunks of ice
and ice spears. They confronted the beast.

The screecher stopped. It hunched down, as if to leap.
They advanced toward it, ice weapons brandished. For a
long moment, the screecher did not move. Then, with a
snarl, it turned and retreated up the valley toward
Qua-orellee.

Qua-orellee *rushed to meet it. It saw him and veered*
away—started up the side of the valley. One of the
people, galloping along in pursuit, headed it off. It swung
back down into the valley, toward Qua-orellee. *Qua-*
orellee *stopped and stood erect, holding his rock high*
above him in both hands.

The beast charged. Its muscles pulsed and slackened
rhythmically. It screamed its rage and savagery. Un-
flinching, Qua-orellee *tensed himself to smash his rock*
down on the beast's skull. He watched the beast surge
toward him, screeching.

Fearlessly, he waited.

3

Ahead, the land loomed in the cold mist, a high mass of darkness rising out of the gray, frosty sea. Hitchcock cringed from it as it rushed overwhelmingly toward him, but then the pilot sent the skimmer sailing toward the crest. Hitchcock looked down dizzily at the crumbling, ice-crusted cliff. Sudden gusts of wind slammed into the small craft. It bucked and jolted, and the pilot fought silently. The engine surged.

Then they were over the land. The winds fell away. Hitchcock saw spread before him a desolate plain of ice and crumbling stone, and beyond, towering high, the white mountains.

But not one living thing.

The pilot twisted around and looked to the man in the midship seat. "Want to check the traps?" he asked. His parka hood was pushed back, and the wind mask dangled from his throat like a bib.

"Yeah," Muller said. He had a snarling voice. "Check 'em. He"—he meant Hitchcock—"he wants to see how we work. But they won't have caught anything."

The pilot nodded, shrugged, and turned front again. The skimmer leaped forward.

Hitchcock lifted his camera. The utter lifelessness of the rock-littered plain was oppressive. It was something the people back home ought to see. This scene, more than any words he could say to them, would impress on them how dreadful Xi Scorpii was.

Muller twisted around to face him. Reluctantly, Hitchcock put down the camera and waited for him to speak.

"We'll see if our traps've caught anything," Muller said. "If they haven't, we'll have to go catch our own."

"What? Do you hunt them?" Hitchcock demanded. The mere idea was appalling.

"We got to get specimens somehow," Muller said.

The skimmer settled down close to the ground and streaked over the plain. The weathered boulders sprawled kaleidoscopically across their path, momentarily slashing at them, then vanished in the distance behind. Ahead, the glacier-choked mountains rose into high, wispy clouds.

"How's it look?" Muller asked. "Pretty bare, huh?" He chuckled. "Wait a couple of months. Right now, it's the tail end of summer."

"Summer?" Hitchcock wondered. Here and there, a few hardy plants dug their roots into chinks in the rock, clinging to existence. Their segmented limbs and stems were frost-burst and coated with rime. Their fleshy, gray-green spines were spread in plaintive supplication to the distant sun.

Tentatively, Hitchcock raised his camera.

"Yeah, summer," Muller repeated. "We get about a whole year of it—one out of four. We're closer to the sun, then. Sometimes the temperature gets up as high as fifteen, here in the tropics—sometimes for weeks at a stretch."

"Only fifteen?" Hitchcock gestured at the rock-strewn, snowless plain. "Why isn't the snow—"

"Fifteen centigrade," Muller explained shortly. "But it just thaws out close to the ocean. The other side of these mountains, there's plenty of snow. You'll see."

The mountains bulked massively over them. The snow-sheathed slopes and bare rock cliffs reared steeply upward like a Titan's wall. For several minutes, the skimmer cruised along that wall, then swung directly toward it where a glacier oozed from a narrow valley down onto the plain.

The glacier's front was like a cliff, sheer and awesome, leaning outward. Berg-sized fragments, broken from it, lay in rubble at its feet. Engine snarling, the skimmer rose before the pebble-pocked wall.

Strong, battering bursts of wind hit the craft as it cleared the edge. Its engine screamed as it forced its way forward into the cold air flowing down from the mountains. Yawning fissures and dark, rippling veins of embedded pebbles streaked past beneath them.

Hitchcock lifted his camera again. The glacier imprinted itself on his tape. "Where are we going?" he asked.

"The other side of the mountains," Muller said. "Where the floppers are."

Hitchcock looked up at the mountains. The valley had curved. Mountains rose skyward all around them.

"But aren't floppers—" How he hated that silly word! "Don't floppers live back there?"

"Not many," Muller said. "That section of coast is cut off from the rest, and there's nothing to live on in winter. Mostly, they stick to the snow country."

"Snow country?" It sounded ominous. "How can they live?"

"They get along," Muller said.

The glacier swelled upward steeply where it squeezed between two mountain ramparts. The skimmer lifted, sailed over the crest, flew on into the heart of the mountains.

"How?" Hitchcock demanded. "What do they live on?"

"They take in each other's wash," Muller told him.

"I don't understand," Hitchcock said.

"They gnaw each other's bones. Put it that way."

The skimmer descended from the mountains to a land of low hills smothered in snow. The sky was cloudlessly blue, and sunlight shimmered blindingly on the frozen, white wasteland. Hitchcock adjusted his camera to minimum sensitivity, to compensate for the glare.

"There it is," Muller said. "Flopper country."

Hitchcock thought of a baron showing off his domain from a castle wall. "Where are they?" he asked.

Muller snorted. "Oh, they're out there. But it's a lot of land, and not many floppers. Our last census put it at about one for every twenty square miles. And without a body-heat spotter, half the time you don't see 'em." He handed Hitchcock a pair of sun goggles.

The skimmer struck out across the rolling land. It stayed high above the hills. "The traps don't signal," the pilot announced. "Check 'em anyway?"

"Naw. Skip it," Muller grumbled. "Just waste our time."

He twisted around to speak to Hitchcock. "Traps don't catch much, these days," he said. "They're getting too smart to get caught."

"Oh?" Hitchcock asked, interested.

"We use pit traps," Muller explained. "Any other kind, they'd be no good in this kind of country. They caught a lot of 'em, a couple hundred years ago. Not any more."

"I see," Hitchcock said. He was almost delighted. At least the creatures weren't completely at the mercy of these men.

"You know what I think?" Muller said. "I think all we ever caught was dumb ones—the smart ones knew enough not to get caught. Now the dumb ones have died out—there's nothing but smart ones left. So we don't catch 'em. Not with traps, anyhow."

"But you catch them?" Hitchcock inferred.

"Yeah. Sometimes," Muller said. He called forward to the pilot. "Head for that place we found all the tracks last week. Maybe they'll still be around."

"How?" Hitchcock asked. "How do you catch them?"

"You'll see," Muller said. He rummaged in a compartment under his feet and brought out a net. He unfolded it and laid it in a long, narrow roll on the cowling beside himself and Hitchcock, up against the cockpit's transparent canopy. He hooked lanyards from the exposed corners to grommets inside the cockpit, just under the rim.

"Dr. Muller," Hitchcock said, almost pleading, "haven't you done *anything* to help these poor creatures? Do you simply let them *live* in this horrible country? And starve? Freeze? Die—?"

"Why not?" Muller wondered. "They're just a bunch of animals."

"Why . . . why it's your human duty," Hitchcock protested, shuddering.

"Look," Muller said with a firm, inflexible patience, "we're scientists. We're here to study these critters— watch 'em and see if they evolve. If we tried to help 'em, we'd mess things up. We couldn't tell what happened naturally and what happened because we made it happen. Anyway, they're no worse off than if we hadn't discovered this planet."

"Dr. Muller," Hitchcock said, condemnation in his tone, "you haven't one spark of humanity in you."

Muller laughed. "Good thing I don't, or I'd be no good here," he said. "Look, mister. These critters have it hard—they've got to live in this country, or they die. And if they live, it's because they've adapted. And if they adapt, it's because they're evolving. Do you want to get in the way of that? Do you?"

"It's indecent!" Hitchcock sputtered. "Criminal! You'd let these poor creatures die and . . . and suffer without lifting a hand! Why, they have the same right to live that you do. I will see them granted that right."

"Go ahead," Muller said. "Just don't interfere with our work. This here's the biggest project in the universe."

"Tracks," the pilot reported.

Hitchcock looked out. Far below, a thin trail threaded across the crest of a low hill and down a steep slope. The skimmer paused and settled groundwards. The trail became the dragging tracks of a clumsy, struggling animal —the flattish footprints close-spaced and scuffed, as if the feet had not been lifted clear of the snow.

"It's a flopper, all right," Muller decided. "Cruise around—let's see if there's more."

The pilot kept them low. They followed the low ridge and crossed several more trails, all of them headed in the same direction. "Looks like a hunting pack to me," the pilot said.

"That's what it is," Muller agreed. And to Hitchcock, "They just started hunting like this about forty years ago. Most of 'em still hunt by themselves, but every once in a while we find signs of 'em working together—like this."

Hitchcock let his camera scan the pattern of tracks in the snow. "Is it significant?" he asked.

"Yeah," Muller said. "They're not gregarious critters. Like I said, most of 'em hunt by themselves. This is the first sign we've had of 'em getting together—they're developing a social sense."

"Civilization?" Hitchcock wondered, awed.

"It's the start of it," Muller said. "Right here."

The pilot had turned the skimmer to follow the hunting pack. Muller pointed down at one of the trails in the snow. "That's the tracks of the thing they're after."

It looked very much like the other trails—slightly messier, with the footprints overlapping in a complicated pattern. Hitchcock gave his camera a long careful look while the skimmer swept up the slope of the low hill and down the other side into the deep valley.

"It's just another sign they're turning smart," Muller said. "Them hunting in packs, I mean. That's evolution working. It takes brains to stay alive in a country like this."

"Do you mean to tell me," Hitchcock wondered, "that *this* is why you refuse to help them—so you can watch their desperate struggles? To . . . satisfy your own curiosity?"

"Sure," Muller said. He sounded satisfied with himself. "Can you think of a better reason? Besides, we may have to fight 'em some day. It'll be a good idea to know all we can about 'em."

"But what possible reason could we have for fighting these . . . these pitiful creatures?" Hitchcock protested.

"If they get smarter than we are," Muller told him, "we *better* fight 'em. And I've got evidence they're going to."

That seemed to settle that. Hitchcock shuddered with horror. For the first time, he could understand Muller's attitude. It troubled him greatly, and he knew it was wrong. He was sure it was wrong. It had to be!

But he, too, was afraid.

The quarry's trail turned to follow the valley. The pilot banked the skimmer sharply to turn after it. "Those tracks look new," he said.

"A couple of hours or less," Muller agreed. The skimmer rocketed down the valley. Hitchcock leaned forward, peering ahead. He held his camera ready to use.

"Are they very far ahead?" he asked.

"Hard to tell," Muller said. "They can move pretty fast when they want to." He pointed to a set of tracks that paralleled the tracks of the quarry. "That boy was using three legs—sort of like an ape when it's running. They do that when they're in a hurry—or else all four."

"They run like *animals?*" Hitchcock asked. He had a

vision of the bumbling, shambling creatures bounding along on all four legs like beasts. The thought was appalling.

The skimmer skidded around the curve of a high, moundlike hill. And there they were. Still far ahead and indistinct in the sun-glare, they were nevertheless unmistakable. Floppers—eight or ten of them.

"Pull back," Muller snapped.

The skimmer bucked and shuddered as the pilot slammed it to a stop against the windblast of its fans. Quickly, they slipped back around the curve of the hill.

"Now you'll see how we do it," Muller told Hitchcock. "Better get buttoned up. It's cold out there." He helped Hitchcock with the unfamiliar clasps of his wind mask, and made sure his parka was zipped tight.

Then he got busy in his own part of the cockpit. Hitchcock leaned forward to see. When he had his own wind mask in place, and his parka was tight, Muller opened the canopy on the side where the net lay rolled on the cowling. A blast of cold air burst into the cockpit. Hitchcock felt it even through his thick clothes. It leaked through his mask and around the brow ridge of his goggles. Painfully, it invaded his nose as he breathed.

Muller pointed to the grommet near Hitchcock's knee, where the net was secured. "Is it tied down good?" he asked. His mask muffled his voice. Hitchcock glanced down negligently and nodded.

Not that he cared if it was tied down properly or not. It was revolting merely to think of using a net to capture a flopper. Such things were unfair—unsportsmanlike.

But Muller accepted the answer. "Let's go!" he barked.

The pilot leaned forward, pushing the control stick all the way front. The skimmer tilted forward. The engine surged.

They skittered around the curve of the hill, then

straightened out and drove. Hitchcock felt the icy wind smash against him. Intense cold leaked through his parka's fastenings. The wind thundered around him. He raised his camera and focused it on the place far ahead where the floppers were gathered. The skimmer hurtled forward like a boat on the crest of a wave.

Muller held a set of binoculars up against his goggles, studying the scene ahead. "They got the thing surrounded," he said. "One of 'em's got a—" He stopped. "Get that one!" he rapped out. "The first one we come to. He's the one we want!"

Hitchcock could make them out, now. A line of floppers was driving a sinuous, short-legged beast toward another flopper. That flopper was standing still, its back to the skimmer. It held something over its head with both of its flipperlike paws. The beast was gliding toward it like a snake.

"That's the one we want!" Muller yelled into the wind.

Muller pushed the rolled net over the skimmer's side. It unrolled and flapped sluggishly in the wind. The skimmer rocked.

They were very close now, and traveling fast. A plume of wind-lifted snow blew up behind them. Hitchcock held his camera fixed on the flopper. The scene exploded into largeness before them.

At the last moment, the pilot spun the skimmer broadside, setting the net to scoop up the flopper. At that instant, Hitchcock reached down and wrenched the net's anchor cord from the grommet near his knee.

Because he was doing that, his camera did not record what followed. The net, robbed of half its support, bunched into a bundle which clubbed the flopper from behind and tumbled it into the snow. A large, ragged, heart-shaped rock flew from its paws.

The skimmer hurtled onward from its own momentum.

The pilot fought to slow it down. Hitchcock raised his camera again.

He got what happened next on the tape—the catlike pounce of the beast, the desperate struggling of the flopper, and the sudden gush of turquoise blood on the white snow.

"You see?" Hitchcock cried triumphantly. "You see? *That's* how you make them live! You murderers!"

4

It was days later that Hitchcock commanded Muller to show how he measured the floppers' intelligence.

Consistently, as his investigation progressed, he had heard their intelligence disparaged. It was a lie and a conspiracy, of course, but he was gradually forced to the realization that the ultimate success or failure of his mission would depend on whether he could turn up evidence to prove they *were* intelligent.

Muller smiled and took him into the laboratory.

At first, what he saw was not encouraging. The problem tests were fantastically simple. In fact, when he tried them, their solutions were practically obvious. But he did force Muller to concede that the floppers could do them, too.

"Yeah, they do 'em," Muller said. "They do 'em almost as good as you do."

Then they came to some problems not so easy. Problems like the fire moat, in which—to reach a scrap of food—the flopper had to cross a wide bed of flame-bright coals.

Baffled, Hitchcock paced back and forth along the edge, his hollow-jowled face made ruddy by the heat. There wasn't any way he could do it. No way at all. Finally, he gave up. "This is impossible," he protested.

"Yeah?" Muller smiled. He walked over, picked up a mat from the floor, and threw it across the hot coals.

"How should I have known it was fireproof?" Hitchcock protested. He was using his camera again, recording the problem and its solution.

"How did you know it wasn't?" Muller answered. "You should have tried it, to find out."

"But you can't expect an . . . an untrained savage to think of *that*," Hitchcock argued.

Muller shrugged. "It's a tough trick, all right," he admitted. "But we've had a few floppers do it."

"Impossible," Hitchcock snapped.

"Not those floppers," Muller said. "They were *smart*."

"What?" Hitchcock wasn't sure he'd heard right. "Not really!"

Muller shrugged and smiled. "We've had a few smart ones."

Hitchcock paused, inwardly jubilant, but he pretended not to be especially impressed. Like a hunter catching sight of his prey, he decided to wait—to bide his time and hope that Muller, unsuspecting, would make further revelations.

The man had the proof he—Hitchcock—needed. That was all he had to know.

There were more problems, most of them even more difficult. Hitchcock managed to solve very few of them, in spite of his heightened vigilance. Muller didn't explain how he expected floppers to solve them, when even a man was baffled. He just smiled.

Hitchcock used his camera to record the ones that

stopped him. If the floppers were considered stupid on the basis of tests like these, it was good proof that they *were* intelligent.

Then they came to the maze problems. Hitchcock blundered through the first simple ones and came out pleased with his own accomplishment but annoyed because he couldn't use them for evidence.

"Well, at least *these* are simple enough," he snapped.

"We just use those to give 'em an idea what a maze is," Muller told him. He conducted Hitchock into another room, where a gigantic panel of signal lights covered a whole wall. He opened a door and motioned Hitchcock inside. Confidently, Hitchcock walked in.

The door clicked behind him. When he turned, there wasn't a sign of where the door had been.

An awful, trapped feeling seized him. He pounded on the wall and shouted. No one answered. The tunnels around him swallowed the sounds without an echo.

He started to run.

Half a minute later, out of breath, he stopped.

This wasn't like the other ones. This one was *hard.*

He looked around. Nothing looked familiar. He couldn't even be sure which way he'd come. He was lost.

Appalled and fearful, he started to search. It was useless. The passageways branched and intersected endlessly. They curved and zigzagged and circled back on themselves. He lost all sense of direction, all sense of distance and time. Trying to retrace his steps, he took a wrong turn. Blank walls stopped him. A down-spiraling tunnel descended to a pool of black, utterly motionless water. Wearily, he turned around and climbed up again.

Then he stopped, breathing hard from the climb. The tunnel forked and other tunnels led off from it. Any one of them could be the right one. Or none of them. Blank-minded, frustrated, Hitchcock lifted his camera and slowly swung it in a full circle.

Let the people back home see this, he thought. Let them see the endless convolutions—the total formlessness of this maze. Let them judge for themselves how well it measured a person's intelligence.

And it was because of things like this they said the floppers were animal-stupid! It was ridiculous. Why, even a man as intelligent as himself couldn't find his way through. The most brilliant man alive couldn't do it.

"Had enough, Hitchcock?" Muller's voice asked.

Startled, Hitchcock whirled. He was completely alone. "Where are you?" he shouted. "Show yourself."

"Had enough?" Muller asked again.

The tunnels twisted around him crazily, shapelessly. A man was a fool to keep trying. He might spend days in this place. Why, he could starve! "Yes! YES!" Hitchcock cried. "Where are you?"

"Wait there," Muller told him. "I'll come get you."

Legs aching with fatigue, Hitchcock slouched against the smooth wall. Why, it was outrageous! The silly rabbit warren didn't even have a place to sit down!

Sigurd Muller came strolling along the passageway less than two minutes later. "How was it?" he asked, smiling raffishly.

Hitchcock straightened up. "How can you believe that this . . . this silly game gives the slightest indication of a person's intelligence? It's absolutely foolish."

Muller chuckled. "I don't know," he said easily. "It gave me a good look at yours."

Hitchcock sputtered. "Young man, no person could possibly find his way out."

"Yeah?" Muller wondered. "Follow me." He jerked a thumb over his shoulder, turned, and walked off.

"But you *know* the way out," Hitchcock protested. He had to scurry to catch up with Muller.

Muller didn't look back. "It isn't easy," he admitted, walking along almost jauntily. "But some people do it the first time through. We've even had some floppers do it."

"Chance," Hitchcock declared, breathing hard to match Muller's pace. "Pure chance."

Muller shook his head. "It wasn't chance," he said. He was very sure. "You don't get through a thing this tricky just with luck. Not fast, you don't. You either just hunt till you hit it, or you think up a method. If you hunt, you're a good long time getting out. But if you're real smart, you think up a method. Those floppers were smart."

"I was told," Hitchcock said pointedly, "that these natives are not intelligent."

"You were, huh?" Muller growled. He shrugged. "They must have been talking about the tame ones that do our muscle work for us. They *are* dumb. So are a lot of the wild ones, but there's been some smart ones, too. There's even been a few so smart none of these tests showed their limits. And that *is* smart. I get scared when I think about 'em."

Then suddenly, they emerged from the maze. Hitchcock stopped and looked around. They were in the same room he had entered the maze from. The door he had gone through was there in the opposite wall.

"Want to try it again?" Muller asked.

"No thank you," Hitchcock snapped. "I've had quite enough of these childish games."

Wryly, carelessly, Muller smiled. "Anything else you want to see?"

"Yes," Hitchcock said. "I want you to show me proof of these intelligent floppers."

Muller nodded cockily. "I figured you would," he said. "I got it all ready for you."

He led Hitchcock from the testing rooms to a small, file-jammed office. The files were a primitive type, as if the scientists here had never heard of memory crystals. Muller bent over the librarian's console and punched out a combination. A folder dropped into the delivery slot.

Muller passed it to Hitchcock, and motioned him to the desk. Hitchcock sat down and spread out the folder's contents. It wasn't an impressive display. The data tables were meaningless. The multicolored photoprints were nothing but abstract designs. Nevertheless, Hitchcock held his camera over them and recorded them slowly, page by page.

Then Muller's shadow fell across the desk. His finger prodded the stacked data pages. "This is how they went through the tests," he said. With a twist of the hand he fanned the sheets out and pulled free a set of seven pages. He laid them on top of the others. "These are how a scientist-candidate scored—I put 'em in to compare with."

Hitchcock separated the four sets of papers and laid them on the desk—the one of the scientist-candidate and three containing the scores floppers had made. He tried to compare the records, glancing randomly from one set to another. But all four were confusingly similar, and the complex mass of numbers, plus and minus signs, and symbols meant nothing to him.

Muller brushed Hitchcock's hands out of the way. He traced a fingertip across the laid-out sequence of the scientist-candidate's scores. Three-quarters of the way through the record, he paused.

"Up to here," he said, "he was even with 'em. They missed a few and he missed a few—they came out even. But from here on—"

His finger traced to the end of the record, then transferred to the corresponding section of the record of one of the floppers. Instantly Hitchcock saw that the two were radically different.

"From here on," Muller continued, "they were way ahead of him—faster and slicker. They didn't miss hardly one. And those jobs were *tough*. Just to give you an idea—" He pointed to a spot not quite halfway through the test sequence. "Here's where *you* pegged out."

Astonished, Hitchcock looked down at the expanse of records. The scientist-candidate must have been a genius to score so far above him. And those floppers—he could not comprehend such intelligence. It didn't matter that he didn't understand the notations or the things they made reference to. Now that it had been pointed out to him, the meaning of those tabulations was plain. He held his camera up and recorded them again.

Muller slapped the photoprints down on top of the papers. "As for these—" he said. "These are brain tissue." He indicated three sheets of eight prints each. "These came from the floppers—the smart ones. And these"—he tapped another set—"are a man's brain. I figured you'd want to compare them, but don't trust it too far—floppers' brains aren't made the same. This one"— he pointed to the fifth set of prints—"is from a normal flopper—one of the boys we keep around to do the work for us."

Hitchcock tried to study the prints—tried to discover the similarities and the differences in them. But his eye was not trained—he didn't know what to look for. The plates were as meaningless as the data sheets had been. Again, Sigurd Muller helped him.

"We use a variable intensity dye," he explained. "Where it's thin, it shows up red—where it's heavy, it's blue. We put it in one cell on each plate."

He tapped one of the prints—the human one—where a blue splotch lay against a pale green-yellow background.

Rootlike arms spread out from the splotch in all directions, branching and rebranching into countless red filaments thinner than hairs.

"That's one brain cell," he said. "Those"—he indicated the arms and the red filaments—"are how it makes connections with the other cells. Put a lot of 'em together and you've got a whole network of connections. This one's different from the others, but all of 'em have connections like that. That's what makes for intelligence —connections."

Hitchcock frowned. These things were difficult to grasp. "Repeat that," he said.

"Take it this way," Muller said. "Intelligence depends on a lot of units being tied up together in a network of communication—a lot of connections and a lot of channels of contact. The smarter you are, the more interconnections you've got, and it's the same the other way around. So there's two ways you can be smart, if you've got a big-enough brain case to start with. You can have ordinary-size brain cells with a lot of these connecting threads, or you can have a lot of cells smaller than normal. Now, look what we've got here."

He tapped the print with the human brain cells on it. "Here we've got normal-size cells with a whole mess of connections." He moved his finger on to the samples from the normal flopper. "This boy was dumb—these pictures are the same scale. The cells are almost as big, and they don't have anywhere near as many contacts."

Hitchcock was using his camera where Muller pointed. He could see that everything was exactly as Muller described it. Muller shifted to the three sets taken from the intelligent floppers. "Now look at these," he was saying.

The cells were much smaller—not half the size of the cells from the normal flopper—and connecting filaments radiated out from them, proliferating endlessly. They looked like spiderwebs.

Hitchcock caught his breath. Why, minds built of cells like these would be incalculably powerful.

Muller smiled at him. "You catch on easy," he said.

"Why, they . . . how magnificent!" Hitchcock exclaimed.

This was the proof he wanted—proof that he was told a lie when he was told the floppers were mindless, dumb animals. Proof—undeniable proof—that the floppers were people, at least insofar as the things that really counted were concerned, people in everything, perhaps, except the shape of their bodies, and that therefore they were entitled to the fundamental rights of all human beings.

But then an unsettling question—a moment of doubt—came into his thoughts. "How . . . how did you obtain these . . . these wonderful specimens?"

Muller snorted. "How do you think? You don't think we'd let 'em run around loose, do you?"

Hitchcock was aghast. "You killed them!"

"Sure," Muller said. "So what? They're only animals."

INTERLUDE

The deadfall had mashed the small animal practically flat, but some of its springy bones flexed back into shape when Kosh-korrozasch levered the ice block off it. He could see what it had looked like.

What he saw astonished him. It was unlike any creature he knew. He tore off a hind leg. A strip of flank peeled off with it. He squatted in the shelter of a rock ledge and gobbled it, bones and all. Then he tore off the other hind leg.

His hunger subsided then. He paused to examine the carcass more slowly. He had thought he knew all the creatures in the world—their shape, their habits, what they could do, and how they tasted. But this was not one of them.

It made him wonder.

A cold wind-gust blasted him, ruffing his pelt. He hardly noticed. He pondered how it was possible an animal could exist anywhere in the world, and he had not seen it till now. Never, till now, had he seen an animal he did not recognize—not since cubhood, when he was freshly come from his parent's pouch.

From his high vantage, here in a cleft where the land reached a narrow white tendril up into the mountains, Kosh-korrozasch looked out at the world. The white, featureless land spread wide and far in the seven directions, and the mountains that surrounded the land were rough and massive—dark, patched with white on their slopes. And there, out in the middle of the land where no mountain belonged, the great, lonely peak rose jaggedly to a flat crest. It was as if one of the monsters that lurked underground had been frozen at the moment it was smashing its way up to freedom.

Kosh-korrozasch had been everywhere in that world, had trod every part of the white, cold land, had searched all the tendrils of land that probed into the mountains— searched all the way to their ends, to where the mountains themselves blocked his way. And he had struggled nearly to the top of the great, lonely peak, there in the middle of the land; he had scraped the scale-food from the rocks up there, on the side where the wind rarely came.

He had learned where there was food in the world, and

where there was none. He had learned how to find it, to trap it, to stalk it, and kill it. He knew all he needed to know about the world, and all the animals in it.

. . . Except this one dead thing his trap had killed. He wrenched the rearward half of the body from the rest of it, and ate it slowly. It was good-tasting food. It filled him with a sense of well-being—of having eaten. Eating was too rare a pleasure. Kosh-korrozasch had been part-starved all his life.

But the creature's strangeness still nagged him. He crumbled the thing's foreleg in his maw, and pondered. It was only then that the thought came to him.

It was a strange thought—strange and frightening. But it excited him, and his paws trembled while he ate the rest of the carcass. He ate slowly, savoring the pleasure of food, feeling the thrill and the wonder of his new thought.

Perhaps there was something beyond the edge of the world. Perhaps the creature had come from there.

Life was hard, here in this world. A being starved all his life and died of hunger. A person spent all his life seeking food, building traps, while the dull ache of hunger gnawed his belly, driving him endlessly on, never satisfied.

Kosh-korrozasch paused when he had finished eating. Using the turquoise blood-dribble of his eating for a bait, he rebuilt the ice-block deadfall. He might never come back here—he knew that—but he might. And if he came back, he might be needing desperately the food it might kill while he was gone.

When it was built, he went away. Climbing upslope, he followed the tendril of land that reached up into the mountains toward the edge of the world. If an animal could enter from outside, perhaps he could leave the same way.

A person searched for food all his life. Slowly, Kosh-korrozasch climbed toward the edge of the world.

5

In thirty-two hours, the supply ship would leave this planet for Lambda Serpentis. Adam Hitchcock felt fine. He would be glad to leave. The dome was like a prison. Outside, the wind was bitter cold and the sea crashed endlessly on the island's rocky shore. The flopper slaves were always underfoot, brainlessly stupid. His quarters had none of the comforts a civilized man was accustomed to, and the food he got was abominably plain.

His endurance had been rudely tested. He was impatient to return to civilization.

But he was satisfied. His mission had been a complete success. He had found out the facts—he knew the truth, and as soon as he returned home everyone would know the truth. The suffering natives would be given, finally, the aid denied them for so long.

And the record of his Society for Humane Practices would remain a record of unblemished success. Truly, he had reason to be proud.

Before he left, though, he had one more task. It was not important—actually a mere formality: to give the scientists a chance to correct the conditions he had exposed. They would refuse him, of course—he expected that; but when they refused, they would lose their right to protest when he aroused public censure against them.

He walked into the office of Ben Reese. Reese, engrossed in a mound of papers, did not see him at once.

"I'm a fair man," Hitchcock stated.

Ben Reese looked up, startled. His paperwork was like a fortress around him. "Did I ever say you weren't?"

Hitchcock went on. "I have proof," he said, "absolute proof—that the natives of this planet are being mal-treated and enslaved, that their needs have been ignored, and that your people have been hounding them to death. Nevertheless, I give you fair warning: if you do not correct these conditions, I shall be compelled to make a public report of my findings. If you force me to do that, I will not be responsible for anything that happens after-ward."

Reese listened in silence. Useless, of course, to quibble over all the realities that Hitchcock had—deliberately?—failed to understand. "We're concerned with scientific research here," he said. "Not welfare. To . . . to do as you demand would mean the end of everything we've worked for, everything we've hoped—"

Doubletalk, of course. Hitchcock had expected that. He wasn't fooled.

"Everything you've worked for!" he echoed. "The deliberate suppression of a people as deserving of human rights as you or I! In clear conscience, I cannot stand by and permit this to go on! I shall—"

Reese raised a placating hand. "That is not true," he protested. He actually seemed embarrassed. "You forget, Mr. Hitchcock—they are animals, not people. Their minds are primitive . . . undeveloped."

"That," Hitchcock said, "is a lie! I have definite proof that they are even more intelligent than men. *Any* men. I say you are deliberately suppressing them because you fear what they could become!"

Gesturing helplessly, Reese said, "I have not seen this evidence."

"Another lie!" Hitchcock accused. He shook his fist. "Do you expect me to believe," he stormed, "that one of your men could have this evidence and you did not know of it? The whole idea is preposterous."

"But I *don't* know of it," Reese insisted. He sounded almost reasonable. "What proof? Where did you get it?"

"Your man in charge of intelligence testing showed me some of his records," Hitchcock said. "And some photographs of brain tissue. They prove conclusively that the floppers . . . that the natives of this planet have minds as good as yours or mine."

Ben Reese was like a man stunned. "I know nothing about this," he protested. "Are you . . . are you sure the evidence really proves that? I mean, perhaps you didn't understand—"

"If Dr. Muller had not helped me," Hitchcock replied, "the evidence would have meant nothing at all."

Reese shook his head. "This is hard to believe," he confessed. "Did he say why he showed you these things?"

"He showed them to me," Hitchcock said, "because I asked him to. He was very cooperative, in spite of his contempt for them, which he made absolutely no attempt to conceal. He said—almost in so many words—that you are doing everything you can to suppress them. He was *proud* of it!"

Reese looked worried. His idle hands, unnoticed, were nervously tearing notepad paper into progressively smaller and smaller bits. A pile of confetti-sized fragments collected on his blotter.

Hitchcock felt a wonderful exhilaration. He had the man totally helpless.

He was about to rise, repeat his ultimatum, and walk out, when Reese turned to the phone at his elbow, saying, "Excuse me a moment. Please."

Without waiting for a reply, he punched out a number. The phone's light blinked. A voice rasped from the speaker.

"Brains department. Muller speaking."

"Sigurd?" Reese asked. "This is Ben. Would you mind coming down here? Something has come up."

"Yeah? Like what?"

"I'd much rather you came down," Reese said mildly. "It's rather complicated."

Muller made an annoyed sound, but then he said, "I'll come." The phone's light went out.

Reese turned back to Hitchcock. "We'll wait till he gets here," he said. "All right?"

Reluctantly, Hitchcock sat back and folded his arms. Scowling, he waited.

This was something he hadn't expected.

Not that it made any difference, of course. Reese was caught in an impossible position. All he could possibly do was try to justify himself.

Hitchcock settled back to wait. He was supremely confident. Just let him try to justify himself. Just let him try!

He could not do it.

6

Ben Reese was deeply troubled. Adam Hitchcock was a well-intentioned fool, and his ability to understand was limited, but Sigurd must have shown him something. Whatever else had happened—whatever else he'd been told—Hitchcock must have seen something. Ben Reese tried to imagine what it could have been. He couldn't. He would have to wait. Sigurd Muller would have to explain. Reese pretended to be busy with his papers. It was the only excuse he could think of not to talk to Hitchcock while they waited. But he couldn't work. There was a lot that still had to be gone over before the *Wayfarer* went back to Lambda Serpentis, but until Muller came and the matter was settled, he could not put his mind to it.

Then Muller walked in, his pointed beard jutting like a prow. He glanced around quickly, noticed Hitchcock, but didn't even pause. "What's up?" he asked jauntily. He grabbed a chair, whirled it around, and straddled it.

Reese put his papers aside. "Mr. Hitchcock tells me the floppers are intelligent," he explained. "That you showed him proof of it."

Muller's eyes shifted from Reese to Hitchcock, then back again. "He did, huh?" he said neutrally.

"This was the first I'd heard of it," Reese said pointedly.

Muller shrugged. "So what?" he said. "If you'd look at the reports I turn in—" He gestured at the papers on the desk.

"I have read your reports," Reese said. "I studied them carefully. You did not mention this development."

"Yeah?" Muller cocked his head, defiant but wary. "Who're you saying that for? Me or him?" He jerked a thumb at Hitchcock.

Reese didn't let himself be steered off. "Do you confirm it?" he asked.

Muller glanced at Hitchcock again before he answered. "Yeah," he admitted. "There's been a few smart ones turn up."

So it was true! Reese wanted to shout with excitement. "How many?" he asked.

"Three," Muller said, holding up fingers. "Three of 'em so smart they scare you. And all from the same country. There's a lot more up there, too—running loose."

"You're sure of that?" Reese asked. It was more than he dared to believe.

"Yeah," Muller said grimly. "There's been a population jump, up there, and everything else has stayed the same. How would you figure it?"

Reese nodded slowly. He sighed. Put together like that, the evidence was good enough—the conclusion was valid. He turned to Hitchcock. "Is this what he told you?"

"Substantially," Hitchcock said.

Reese turned back to Muller. A suspicion had grown in him, ugly and fearful. Now he had to destroy it—or see it confirmed.

"He tells me you showed him test records," he said. "And photos of brain tissue. Were they authentic?"

"Sure they're authentic," Muller said. "You think I'd fake a thing like that? Look—all I did was show him around, and show him how we work, and I answered his questions and let him see everything he wanted to see. You got any objections to that?"

Reese shook his head. "To that? No," he conceded. "But these brain-tissue samples—I presume you took them from the different sections of their brains."

"I know how to take specimens," Muller said.

Reese felt sick and old. "You killed them," he said. "All three."

"Right." Muller smiled with clenched teeth, fiercely proud of himself.

"Sigurd," Reese said, "you've done a terrible thing." He turned to Hitchcock again.

"I wish this hadn't come out while you were here," he said. "I can only say that I heard nothing about these intelligent ones until now, and that Sigurd killed them without my knowledge. If I had known, I would have stopped him. He acted against regulations and against our policies. I am grateful to you for exposing him."

Muller shot to his feet, his hands fisted. "Exposing me!" he snarled. "Why you little—"

With an effort, Reese kept his voice even. "You may go now, Sigurd," he said. "I . . . I suggest that you start packing. You have"—he glanced at the clock—"thirty hours before the ship leaves. If anyone asks, tell them that you resigned, and that I accepted your resignation."

Rage burned on Muller's face. He hurled the chair out of his way and walked up to the desk until it bumped his knees. "You don't make a goat of me that easy," he threatened through his teeth. He jerked a thumb at Hitchcock. "What about him? You can't shut *him* up. What are you going to do? Pat him on the head and tell him to be good?"

Reese glanced at Hitchcock. There was a firmness of decision on the man's hollow-jowled face—a look of holy purpose about his eyes. As he watched, the man rose to his feet with solemn dignity, a bone-lean figure clad in black.

"You're a very clever man, Mr. Reese," he said. He spoke slowly. "But not clever enough. You cannot deny the things I have seen with my own eyes. Nor can you lay all the blame at the feet of your underlings. What this man has done"—he gestured at Muller—"has no bearing on the fundamental fact that the welfare of this planet's natives has been willfully and shamefully ignored—and that you have refused to do anything about it. If you do not correct this situation at once, I will expose you to every civilized community in the universe!"

"But you don't understand," Reese protested.

"I have not yet finished," Hitchcock snapped. "In addition, if you still refuse, we—my Society for Humane Practices and I—shall do it ourselves. We shall sponsor a public subscription. We shall send food, clothes—all the things these poor people need. As many shiploads as necessary. And we shall see that you and all your scientists are removed from this planet. Your presence here will not be tolerated."

"Have you any idea how much it would cost?" Reese wondered.

"The cost is not important," Hitchcock said. "The public will gladly pay whatever is needed."

Reese conceded the point. The knowledge that he could not win against this man was strong in him. It paralyzed his will. He wished he were a woman, or a child, so he could retreat into the weakness of frustrated tears.

"You've done this sort of thing before, haven't you?" he said, remembering what he had heard of Hitchcock's doings on other worlds.

"I have," Hitchcock said. "I have been very successful at it." He paused, waiting for Reese to speak. Reese said nothing.

"If you have nothing more to say—" he said. He turned toward the door.

Desperately, then, Reese spoke.

"Only this," he said with a firmness he did not feel. Hitchcock turned back and faced him. He tapped a finger on the desk. "I gather from what Sigurd has said that some floppers may be intelligent," he said. He spoke carefully, deliberately. "Some, but not all. In fact, speaking in terms of the entire planetary population, only a very few are intelligent. All the rest are still animals."

Hitchcock was not impressed. "All of them need our help," he said. "We cannot and we shall not give it to some and deny it to others, no matter what criterion you propose. I can think of nothing so unthinkable."

"The point I'm trying to make," Reese said patiently, "is that . . . that the floppers are in a period of transition. Right now, only some of them are intelligent—only a few. But some day, all of them will be intelligent, because . . .

because they are living under arduous conditions, and the intelligent ones are better able to survive—the population increase Sigurd mentioned is evidence of that. So, comparatively speaking, a greater proportion of the intelligent ones will survive to maturity. And the mature ones will tend to live longer than . . . than the ordinary ones—so they will tend to produce more young. It's a perfect example of the natural selection process. But it *won't* happen if we try to help them."

"What?" Hitchcock shouted. "Preposterous!"

"It . . . it's very true," Reese assured him. "You see, if we gave them everything they need, the intelligent ones wouldn't have an advantage over the ordinary ones— they'd all have an equal life expectancy. And the ordinary ones outnumber the intelligent ones by a fantastic margin, so—even if the intelligence gene-complex is a dominant—the intelligent ones would be absorbed into the race within a few generations. There wouldn't be anything left of them."

Hitchcock appeared to consider the argument, but his face was set stubbornly. Bitterly, Reese wondered if the man understood a thing he'd said.

Then Hitchcock spoke. "Am I to conclude, then," he said, "that you *want* the natives to suffer? To starve? To . . . to *die?* To battle each other for a scrap of food? Do you admit that this is what you want?"

He had understood part of it, Reese concluded glumly. The ugly part. "I think it is necessary," he had to admit. "I think it is the only way the floppers can advance. Remember, something like this must have happened to our own ancestors. If it hadn't, we would still be mindless brutes."

"Nonsense," Hitchcock said. "The fact that our ancestors had no one to help them has nothing to do with it. They would have become men no matter what happened.

It was their *destiny* to become men—and that same destiny exists for these poor people here. Nothing can possibly stand in their way—no man can interfere with destiny. They are suffering and dying because you deliberately neglect their welfare. You have the power to end that suffering and you are morally bound to do it. To refuse, Mr. Reese, is to turn your back on humanity."

Reese sat perfectly still, a feeling of blind hopelessness crushing down on him. "I think," he said slowly. "I think I know why Sigurd helped you so much." Only as he spoke the name did he realize that Muller had not yet gone. "He wants to suppress the intelligent ones. Am I right, Sigurd?"

"Sure I want 'em kept down," Muller snapped. "We'd better, if we know what's good for us. You've seen the wild ones—they're a bunch of animals. Nothing they'd like better than to tear a man apart and eat the pieces."

"On the other hand," Reese put in thoughtfully, "the ones here in the outpost are docile."

Muller disparaged the point with a wave of the hand. "They don't count," he claimed. "They're way off the main track. It's the ones on the mainland that count. If we let *them* get smart, there'll be no stopping 'em. They'll hunt us down. *We'll* be the animals! If we don't stop 'em, they'll chase us right out of the universe. Right now, we can stop 'em. Later on it'll be too late. So we'd better get at it. Right now."

He really believed it, Reese realized. He meant every word of it.

"Sigurd, I don't agree," Reese said. He hoped he sounded reasonable. "In the first place, we conducted some personality experiments on them about twenty years ago. We took the offspring of wild floppers and raised them with our tame ones. They developed none of the . . . the bloodthirsty traits of their parents. So I'm sure that this . . . this viciousness we see in them is a characteristic forced on them by their environment."

"Yeah?" Muller scoffed. "But the smart ones aren't growing up here in the dome. They're growing up out there—on the mainland."

Reese nodded. "True," he admitted. "But before they could be any danger to us, they would have to develop a civilization—a technology. And one of the characteristics of a technological civilization is the ability of its people to control their environment. By removing the causes of their viciousness, they would also remove the need for being vicious. Also, I believe they have shown this same viciousness toward each other—to the point of cannibalism. But recently, I understand, some of them have taken to hunting in groups. They have discovered the advantages of cooperation. Don't you think this shows a trend away from . . . from animal savageness? Don't you, Sigurd?"

"You want to take a chance on it?" Muller asked.

"Taking that chance is the only honorable thing we can do," Reese told him.

"Huh!" Muller snorted. "And how do you think they'll look at us, once they get smart, with us sitting here not doing a thing to help 'em? They'll hate us. They'll hate us like hell!"

Reese hesitated, then shook his head. "No, Sigurd," he decided. "The transition will be a slow, very gradual process. It will be all right to start helping them long before they could become a danger to us. Also, if they do become as intelligent as you say, they will probably understand that they could not have evolved to intelligence if we had tried to help them."

Muller snorted. "You're doing a lot of supposing," he

said. "Suppose you're wrong? It's the whole future of the human race you're talking about, you know. That's . . . that's *us!*"

Reese nodded. "I know," he admitted placidly. "Whatever we do—whatever we decide—it will be thousands of years before the consequences come. I rather imagine we'll have been forgotten. That puts a terrible responsibility on us. We must try to do what is right."

"And on that basis you refuse to help them?" Hitchcock demanded. "Mr. Reese, I have never heard such a preposterous—!"

So all his efforts at persuasion had failed. Reese slumped in his chair, his arms on the rests. He wondered what to do. Muller's careful half-truths, Hitchcock's stubborn ignorance, together they were too much to fight. He could do nothing. He was helpless. Defeat and frustration wearied him, and he felt a sick pity for all the intelligent floppers who would now never be born.

It wasn't fair. It just wasn't fair.

But he did not say it. Thinking it to himself, he realized how futile it was to speak of fairness to these men. And besides, by what right could he ask for fairness—an ideal—from the real world?

Of course it wasn't fair. Nothing was ever completely fair in the real world, because the real world conformed to the physical laws, not the rules of sportsmanship and fair play. It was a hard, bitter thought to accept, but Ben Reese accepted it. As a scientist, he had to accept it no matter how he felt about it.

And in that recognition, he saw, was the key—the way he could protect the floppers from both these men.

He turned to his phone again. "You will excuse me, won't you?" he requested politely as he punched the number combination. His hand trembled.

Before either Hitchcock or Muller could nod their

assent, someone answered the phone. "Clinic," he said. "Nick?" Reese guessed. "This is Ben. Could you send up a couple of your boys?"

"Sure," said the one identified as Nick. "But what—?"

"Never mind," Reese said quickly. "Just send them." He broke the connection.

"What's the matter?" Muller wanted to know. "You feel sick?"

Reese ignored the question. "I've changed my mind, Sigurd," he said. "You can stay here."

Muller backed up a step. "Well, now, I don't know," he said warily. He scratched his beard. "I've been here a long time—"

"But, Sigurd," Reese urged, "we're going to need you here—at least for the next year. All the information you've held back—"

"It's in my files," Muller said. "You'll find it, if you want it bad enough." He moved toward the door. "I'm going to pack." In a moment, he was gone.

Reese smiled a complacent smile. "There'll be no room for him in the ship," he confided to no one in particular. He leaned forward. "As for you, Mr. Hitchcock . . . sit down, please. There's one thing more I want to say."

Hitchcock paused uncertainly, then resumed his chair. "Let it never be said," he declared, "that I will not hear all arguments."

Reese nodded, pleased. Everything would be all right if he could keep Hitchcock in his office until the boys came from the clinic. "Mr. Hitchcock," he said, "in a sense, I'm very glad you came."

Hitchcock scowled.

"For one thing," Reese went on, "it was you who . . . who brought out the fact that the floppers are developing intelligence. If you hadn't come, Sigurd might have concealed it for years. Of course, Sigurd was hoping you'd help him to . . . to wipe out the intelligent ones, but that is beside the point."

"Mr. Reese," Hitchcock said, "you cannot convince me that black is white."

"Oh, of course," Reese agreed. "But there are hundreds of shades of gray. The other reason I'm glad you came"— he spoke earnestly—"you've forced me to re-examine what we're doing here—to . . . to question the rightness of our doing nothing about the conditions in which the floppers live. It's not an easy thing to be sure of."

"So you admit it!" Hitchcock was triumphant. "You admit—"

Reese silenced him with a gesture. "No," he said firmly, "I do *not* admit it. I have come to the same conclusions I have always held. But now—because of you—I know *why* it is right."

"Impossible," Hitchcock objected. "It is *not* right."

Ben Reese was very patient with him. He could afford to be patient—it used up time, while the boys from the clinic were coming.

"You're a very moral man, Mr. Hitchcock," he said. "I'd be the first to admit it. But, unfortunately, a high moral sense is not enough. You see, Nature *isn't* moral— it doesn't conform to our concepts of right and wrong, and it isn't limited to conditions where the right and wrong of a matter are easy to decide. There are times when an act that seems morally right can lead to . . . to something horrible. You cannot say a thing is morally right or wrong until you've considered the context in which it happens. And that, Mr. Hitchcock, is where your moral sense fails you."

"I do not need a scientist to tell me the difference between right and wrong," Hitchcock said.

Reese nodded pleasantly. "I expected you'd say that. But you're wrong. Until you know the consequences of an act, you cannot tell whether or not it is moral. And there are times—such as now—when a layman like yourself does not understand the forces involved. When that happens, you cannot predict the consequences of an act. Therefore, you cannot decide whether it is right or wrong."

"You're wrong!" Hitchcock insisted. "The end *never* justifies the means! *Never!*"

Reese didn't deny it. He said, reasonably, "On the other hand, there are times when no other test applies—when all the possible courses of action look equally bad. And even when you can do something which seems absolutely right, you still have to think of the consequences. If the consequences are bad, the act itself must be bad. Or suppose there is a . . . a morally imperative goal which you can achieve only by doing things which any moral code would condemn?"

Hitchcock was incredulous. "Such a thing could not happen."

"I am talking," Reese said firmly, "about now. About the situation here. That is the problem we have been dealing with here, ever since this station was built— whether to help them, give them comfort and security, and destroy for all time their hope of ever becoming more than animals—or whether we should let nature take its course, allow many to die, and many more to suffer, so that some day their descendants can stand before us as equals."

He shrugged expressively. "We can do only one thing. We must balance the wrong we know we are doing against the goal we are morally obliged to support. We must go ahead and . . . and try not to let our consciences upset us too much."

"If you must rationalize a thing," Hitchcock said, "it's wrong. Good does not come from evil!"

Reese shrugged helplessly. "We must do what we think is right," he said. "And if our judgments are different from someone else's, we must follow our own. We—"

He broke off as the door opened. Two floppers came in, wheeling a stretcher. Each one had a big red cross dyed in the fur on its chest.

Reese pointed at Hitchcock. "That man is sick."

The floppers advanced, their resilient feet rustling softly on the floor. Hitchcock, taken aback by Reese's abrupt statement, thumbed his chest. "Me?"

The floppers came up, one on each side of him. They grabbed his arms close to the shoulder. Hitchcock yipped with surprise, turned his head, and found the solicitous, repulsive face of a flopper only inches from his own.

With a strangled, terrified cry, he lunged from the chair. The floppers kept him from falling headlong on the floor. Wild-eyed, he struggled to get loose from them, but they held on. He kicked at them desperately. They dragged him backward. His feet flailed the air.

"Make them let me go!" he yelled. "Make these filthy monsters let me go!"

Reese sat back and relaxed. He was sorry he had to do this to the man, but it did somehow give him a pleasant feeling.

It was not, after all, as if Hitchcock was a really good man.

"I'm afraid I can't do that," he said. "They've been taught to take a sick man to the clinic. I couldn't stop them now if I wanted to." He spread his hands helplessly. "As I've said before, they're rather stupid."

One of the floppers moved behind Hitchcock and held both his arms. The other flopper took an ampule from the pouch on its harness. Hitchcock stared at the shiny needle with the fascination of sheer terror. "Don't let him!" he screamed. "Don't let him! It's murder!"

The flopper peeled Hitchcock's sleeve up and stabbed the needle into the fleshy part of his arm. Hitchcock uttered a faltering cry, shuddered, and sagged.

"Oh, it's only a mild sedative," Reese said cheerfully. "We wouldn't dare trust them with anything stronger. But you shouldn't have struggled so much."

Hitchcock hung laxly in the flopper's arms. His eyes had a glassy look. The floppers wrapped a blanket tightly around him. His mouth moved as if he was trying to speak, but no words came out.

"The ship is going to leave without you," Ben Reese said. "I'm sorry about that, because I don't think I'm going to enjoy your company for the next year. We'll tell them . . . I think we'll tell them you're sick. A . . . a local disease—one we don't want to spread on other planets. There aren't any diseases like that, of course, but that doesn't matter."

He was very apologetic about the whole thing.

Hitchcock was making apoplectic noises now. "Outrage! Criminal! I'll have the law on you!" For a man of firm moral fiber, some of his comments were remarkably unprintable.

Ben Reese shrugged. "I'm afraid there isn't any law here," he said. "We didn't need any, till you came along. I . . . I'm sorry we have to do this to you, but—well, we can't let you go back to Earth. You'd agitate to have our charter revoked and . . . and then you'd organize this gigantic interstellar aid program, and destroy the floppers' only hope of ever being anything more than animals. We . . . we just can't let you do that."

By this time, Hitchcock was wrapped in the blanket like a mummy. Gently, the floppers lifted him and laid him in the cradlelike stretcher. "You won't get away with this!" he warned.

The floppers fumbled deftly with the straps, securing

him. Their digitless hands were remarkably dexterous. All Hitchcock could move was his head and his mouth.

"Oh, we'll have to let you go next year, of course," Reese admitted. He wasn't disturbed by the thought. "But that is a whole year away. We'll have plenty of time to prepare the public for you. If we give them the whole truth now, I rather doubt they'll be much impressed with your partial truths later on. I'll send instructions about that to our business office on Lambda. Just to announce that the floppers are beginning to evolve should be a good start, and—"

He smiled. He felt wonderful. Perhaps treating Hitchcock this way *was* lousy and unethical, but even Hitchcock himself would have to admit that, everything considered, it was definitely a moral act.

The floppers began to wheel Hitchcock out of the room. Hitchcock was raving.

"You can't do this to me!" he protested. "You can't!"

"Really?" Ben Reese knew it was cruel, but the temptation was too strong.

"Really, Mr. Hitchcock," he said, "I *must* have proof."

EPILOGUE

Slowly, the procession marched past the bier of the Dead One, who was nameless because he was dead, and who had been their leader. Each one, as he came to the bier, crouched low in obeisance, then moved on. The shaman stood over the bier, his pelt stained green to signify that he personified the Dead One. He acknowledged each obeisance by raising his arms.

Shokk-elorrisch stood beside the bier, and he also

acknowledged the obeisances, for he was the new leader in the Dead One's stead. Already, he held the tool-stone in his hand, and he chanted the four harsh, many-toned syllables of the ritual. "My eyes shall find the path for your feet," he said. "My hand shall feed you and my pelt shall warm you. I am all of you. I give you my self."

This he spoke to each one who made obeisance to him, and each one responded: "Show me the path!"

The procession shuffled on, and formed ranks beyond the bier. And when the last one made his obeisance, the three eldest-born from the Dead One's body came forward. They lifted the vine-woven sling which cradled the Dead One. Shokk-elorrisch flanked them on one side and the shaman on the other. All of them chanted: "You are all of us; your eyes saw the path; your hand fed us; your pelt warmed our bodies. We are grateful; we honor you; we sanctify the memory of you; we give you back to yourself!"

Chanting this, their tread matched to the chant, they advanced to the edge of the cliff. There they stopped, and the cadenced rhythm of their chant broke with the cry, "We cast you out!" and they hurled the Dead One into the foaming sea. And the sons of the Dead One and the shaman turned to Shokk-elorrisch. They made obeisance to him, and they said: "Show us the path!"

But Shokk-elorrisch did not answer, nor did he show them any sign that he heard. Standing at the cliff edge, the wind rippling his pelt and the waves crashing on rocks far below, he faced out to sea and made obeisance to the God Ones who lived in the round mountain, there on the island that rose from the horizon—the God Ones, who never had to migrate in search of new hunting ground, and who watched from the boulder that floated like a cloud in the wind—who watched but took no part in the things they witnessed.

And he wondered, even as he made obeisance to them, why they kept themselves aloof, and what was the source of their powers, and whether his people, too, could achieve those powers—to become the equals of those strange and enigmatic beings.

And he wondered, too, would they teach him? Would they teach him if he went to that mountain—out there at the edge of the sky? Would they permit him to learn the secret of their powers?

He wondered how to cross those tattered waves—how to climb that shore and ascend to the crest of that mountain.

Thinking thus, Shokk-elorrisch knew what his path would be. And the path of his people.

Toward greatness. Toward the mastery of Nature.

Toward glory.